By Aileen Fisher

Cover Design by Elle Staples

Cover illustration by Tatiana Glebova

This unabridged version has updated grammar and spelling.

Originally titled *Cherokee Strip*

First published in 1956

© 2018 Jenny Phillips

Table of Contents

Chapter 1: Heading for the Promised Land 1

Chapter 2: Upsetting News 19

Chapter 3: Bad Luck at Caldwell 36

Chapter 4: Becky Gets an Idea. 52

Chapter 5: New Hope. 68

Chapter 6: On Your Mark! 83

Chapter 7: Get Set – Go! 99

Chapter 8: The Disputed Claim. 116

Chapter 9: Home, Sweet Home 137

CHAPTER 1

Heading for the Promised Land

The Fletchers' camp-site in Kansas wasn't much different from the last one in Missouri, but Becky couldn't help feeling excited. Their covered wagon was twenty-five miles closer to the Promised Land!

She turned dreamy gray eyes on the dusty grass beside the road. The Kansas ground was thirsting and yearning for rain, same as the Missouri Ozarks they'd left behind. Early September heat pressed down from all directions, even though the sun was dipping toward the fringe of trees in the west. Would it be like this when they got to Oklahoma Territory, Becky wondered? When they got to the Race for the Prairie?

"Dreaming, daughter?" Becky's father called. "Did you give Sprinter his oats?"

Becky flipped back a stray lock of brown hair and turned quickly to the wagon to unhook a battered tin pan from its place under the washtub. "Just a-doing it, Pappy."

"Got to keep Sprinter in first-class condition for the race, you know."

Yes, she knew. Everything depended on Sprinter. With Pappy a-riding him, he'd pull ahead of the other horses jammed along the starting line. He'd race for all he was worth when the gun went off at 12 o'clock noon on the 16th day of September. He'd find the Fletchers one of the best homesteads in the Race for the Prairie.

Becky hurried toward Sprinter with the pan of oats. With her free hand she rubbed the white streak down the front of the horse's nose. "You've got to run like mad, Sprinter," she urged, for the hundredth time. "You've got to find us a choice quarter section. None of that thin rocky land like the farm we left in Missouri."

Sprinter munched his oats without blinking an eye. His sleek, black sides gleamed.

"You've got to beat the others all hollow, you and Pappy," Becky said. Proudly she ran her hand around one of Sprinter's ears, then around the other. "If we didn't have you, Pappy would have to ride one of the mules in the race. And where'd he get on a mule?"

Sprinter curled his velvet lip over the last oats in the pan.

"Only five or six more days, old boy, and we'll reach Arkansas City. And that's as far as we have to go in Kansas to be across from some of the best land in the Strip." Becky gave Sprinter a final pat and checked his rope and picket pin carefully. It wouldn't do to have Sprinter break loose, not with the greatest race in history only two weeks away.

That's what everyone said it would be—the greatest race in history! "Come September 16, 1893, we'll see the biggest hoss race in the world," folks said. "Nearly six-and-a-half million acres of land for settlement. Why, that's as big as the whole state of Vermont. Far and away bigger than the state of Massachusetts. It's even bigger than Connecticut, Delaware, and Rhode Island put together! Come September 16, we'll see the last great run for cheap land. The last frontier!"

Becky turned back to the covered wagon, filled to overflowing with the Fletchers' possessions. All they had left in the world! They'd had to leave the heavy, bulky things behind, like Gran's spinning wheel, and the heirloom dresser with the cracked mirror. Matt had cried when Pappy said there wasn't room for his hobbyhorse. And tears had run down Dave's cheeks when he said goodbye to the old collie. Becky couldn't help thinking how lucky she was that her prized possession was small enough to keep in her pocket.

She walked slowly through the grass, seeing but hardly noticing her father raising the tent and her mother and the two boys laying a wood fire between flat stones.

"Dig out the sorghum jug, Becky," her mother called. "It's wrapped in a gunny sack inside a kettle. And mind you don't pull out the vinegar instead."

"Sorghum!" Ross Fletcher sniffed, and winked at his daughter. He was heaving off the chicken coop tied to the back of the wagon. There would still be time before dark for the chickens to stretch their legs and peck around under young Matt's watchful eye.

"Think black sorghum. You needn't be too mindful of the jug, daughter. We'll be making sweet'ning out of watermelon juice when we're a-living in the Promised Land.

"When we're a-living in the Promised Land!" cried ten-year-old Dave, never tired of hearing of the wonders that lay ahead. "What else will we be having?"

Becky saw her mother look up quickly from the cornbread batter she was stirring. "We'll grow some wheat for making white-flour bread," she said confidently. "White-flour bread 'stead of cornbread all the time."

"White-flour biscuits with sweet'ning on," Dave sang out.

"And not just for company when folkses come?" Matt asked, big-eyed.

Becky was listening, holding the sorghum jug. She wasn't the only one in the family cherishing hopes…

"What you a-thinking, Becky?" her father asked.

Ever since leaving their rocky, run-down Missouri farm, four days before, Becky had let her hopes grow into rainbows. She didn't know where to start telling what she thought. How could a body pick out a piece of rainbow when it was all so shining-bright?

She put down the jug and poked at some sticks that had fallen from the campfire. The lid to the Dutch oven was heating in the fire. When the blaze died down to coals, her mother would bake the cornbread in the Dutch oven buried in embers, with the hot lid on upside down to hold coals.

"I'm thinking of more than sweet'ning and white-flour bread," Becky said slowly. "I'm thinking of 160 acres of our own picking, without a hungry mortgage to eat up the earnings. I'm thinking of leaving hard times behind."

She didn't come right out and say that she was thinking mainly of things for herself. A house big enough so she could have a room all her own. A new pair of shoes, instead of Mrs. Brant's too narrow hand-me-downs. A boughten dress instead of always made-overs, and a silver bowknot pin like the one Pappy had given Ma when they were married. But they were all part of her rainbow.

"Can't expect our vines to hang with grapes overnight, though," her mother warned. "That's not the way of nature, even on the best soil in Oklahomy Territory."

Ross Fletcher nodded. "First we'll have the sod to break. Then we'll have the seed to sow. We won't be a-gathering in the harvest overnight."

"We won't be paying Old Brant twelve percent interest on a big mortgage, anyway."

She saw her father's face harden. Ross Fletcher and Old Brant had never lost any love on each other, and when her father felt that way about somebody, Becky did, too. "We'll be paying only four percent on the $400 it will take to get the best land in the Race for the Prairie. And didn't you say, Pappy, there's already a move on to have the government cancel the mortgages, so the land will be free and clear?"

Becky saw hope light up her mother's face, above her faded blue calico collar. "Free and clear, like the first Indian Territory land opened up four years ago."

"There's already a move on to cancel the purchase mortgages," Ross Fletcher nodded, "but it may take years."

A covered wagon pulled by a yoke of oxen came

lumbering down the road. A man and boy walked beside the oxen—a long-legged boy who looked to be about fifteen—Becky's own age—for all he was so tall. She had noticed the boy and wondered about him when they had passed the wagon a while back on the road.

"Whoa!" the man shouted, as the oxen drew up. He waved at Ross Fletcher. "You folks camping here tonight?"

"I reckon so."

"Mind if we join you, the lad and me?"

"Glad to have you, stranger."

"We're hankering for a bit of company after a long slow drive," the man explained.

"I've just put cornbread batter in the Dutch oven," Becky's mother called out, friendly-like. "We'd be pleased to have you eat with us."

"Thank you, ma'am."

Becky scuffed in the dust with her bare toes. That was like Mama! Always ready to give a handout to someone, though the Fletchers never had overmuch for themselves. She'd open one of her best jars of blackberry preserves, no doubt. And who'd picked the berries, out in the hot sun and brambles? She hadn't picked all those berries just to feed passing strangers.

Maybe Old Brant was right, in spite of what Granny Fletcher said. As Becky watched the man and boy unyoke the oxen, her fingers closed around the cartridge-shaped pencil in the pocket of her gingham skirt. From one end of the gold cartridge she could pull a short pencil with a red lead; from the other end a short pencil of blue. She had got it from Old Brant... and there wasn't another pencil like it in all of Missouri. Nor would there be in all the Race for the Prairie. It was her prized possession. The pencil, at least, was all her own and not for sharing.

The Brants had lived in the best house in the district, back in Missouri. A white house with columns, at the end of a shady lane. Behind the house were stables, and horses. More than once Mr. Brant had said, as he paid her for doing some chore or other; "You've got to think of yourself first, Becky Fletcher. First, last, and always. You can't ever get ahead thinking of someone else."

Well, the Fletchers hadn't got ahead.

On the other hand, there was Granny, with her bright blue eyes always a-dancing and a-darting. "Who'd want to be like Old Brant, Becky? For all his money he hasn't a friend in the world. 'Tain't money or things bring happiness, I can tell you. 'Tain't money or things." That's what Granny used to say.

Lifting her eyes, Becky saw the boy coming back from turning the oxen out to graze. He had an expectant look, a sort of lonesome-like, hopeful look. His overalls were frayed at the hem and patched at the knees and too short for him. Likely he had no womenfolk to fix them.

Becky relented and smiled. "You like to fish?" she asked.

The boy smiled back, and his nose wrinkled so the freckles all came together. "I sure enough do."

"There's a creek over there, looks like," Becky said, nodding toward the line of trees. "Might be we could catch some fish while the cornbread's baking."

The boy hesitated. "I'll be having to help Pa set up camp first, though."

"No, you run along, Oren," the boy's father urged. "You run along for once. I'll take care of things."

Becky snatched the fish line, hooks, and sinkers her father kept handy at the back of the wagon, and she and the new boy started for the creek. "Grab yourself a few grasshoppers for bait as you go along," she said. "Where you from?"

"Missouri. Lawrence County."

"That's not very far away, is it? I recollect we saw a sign when we drove through."

"It's not far but it took us three days to get this far, with the oxen," Oren answered.

"We're from the Ozarks, Dallas County," Becky said. "We've been on the way four days, driving mules."

"They're faster than oxen. Wish we had mules, or horses. If we get fifteen miles a day with our critters, we're lucky."

"Where're you heading?" Becky asked.

"Caldwell, Kansas."

"That's on the other side of Arkansas City, isn't it?"

Oren nodded. "We're going to make the Run into the Strip from Caldwell."

"The Run! You going to make the Run?" Becky slowed down. "So are we—from Arkansas City. Why are you going clear to Caldwell?"

"Pa thinks it won't be as crowded. He thinks we'll have a

better chance from there. And the land's cheaper…"

"But the best land in the Strip is south of Arkansas City," Becky interrupted.

"It costs more, though. Two dollars and fifty cents an acre. It's only $1.50 south of Caldwell. You can get a homestead for $240."

"We're a-going to get one of the best homesteads in Oklahomy," Becky said confidently. "Sprinter will see to that."

"Sprinter?"

"Our horse. One of the best running horses you ever did see."

"You mean you've got a good fast horse to make the Run?" Oren couldn't keep the envy out of his voice.

"They don't come any better than Sprinter. With Pappy in the saddle, we're bound to get us a choice piece of land." Her voice fell a little as she added, "The rest of us will have to wait in Arkansas City with the wagon and mules… till Pappy stakes his claim and files on it at the land office. Then we'll all move in."

"Wish we had a fast horse," Oren sighed. "Wish we could be in there at the front of the race, 'stead of tagging along behind with the oxen."

They were at the creek now, and Becky looked expertly around for a sapling to break off for a fish-pole.

Oren stood watching. "How'd you get a fast running horse like that Sprinter?"

"Well…" Becky hesitated.

"Must have cost a lot of money. How speedy is he? Has he ever won a real race?"

"He took a blue ribbon at the county fair for the last three years straight. For the best horse in his class."

"Must have cost a lot of money," Oren said.

"He didn't cost Pappy anything," Becky answered. Then, seeing the puzzled look on Oren's face, she added, "It's hard to explain. We didn't have in mind getting the horse."

"Then how'd you get him?"

"Well, it was after Mr. Brant died. Old Brant had the best horses in Dallas County. You see, my mother took care of his wife when she was sick one time. That must have been twenty years ago. Before I was born anyway and I'm the oldest in our family. Nobody thought Mrs. Brant would pull through, but she did. My mother nursed her night and day for weeks and weeks."

Becky ran her eye up and down a clump of black willows, and tested one for strength. Oren waited.

"Old Brant never paid my mother a cent," Becky went on. "Not that she wanted pay, anyway. Not for a thing like that. Not my mother."

"How'd you get the horse?" Oren insisted.

"Well… Mr. Brant died this summer, just two weeks after my Granny Fletcher. Mrs. Brant knew we were a-wanting to make the Run into the Strip if we could sell our place for enough to pay off the mortgage and get out clear. So when Pappy sold, she called Mama and me over. Said she'd always been no end grateful to Mama for saving her life that time, and to me for helping out with housework and coming to feed the horses when her husband took sick. But she hadn't been able to do anything about it, 'long as her husband was alive.

"Said, as token of her feeling, she wanted us to have Sprinter, so we wouldn't miss out getting a good homestead. Said there wouldn't be any better horse on the starting line and I know she's right."

"Likely soundin' hoss story," a voice drawled from a nearby clump of bushes. "Gettin' a hoss withouten a bill o' sale."

Becky and Oren drew back as the bushes parted and a lanky man came out on the bank. He walked with a slight stoop, as if wanting to hide some of his height. There was a lump of chewing tobacco in his cheek and a brown stain at the corner of his mouth.

"I seen you campin' yonder by the road," he said. "Been watchin' you. Seen you comin' here toward my property, stealin' my timber."

Becky eyed the piece of willow in her hand. "Timber? This skinny little fish-pole?"

"Ain't no fish in this here creek," the man went on. "So you can get right back to where you come from. I don't want no kids breakin' down my timber."

Flushing, Becky threw down the willow sapling. "Come on, Oren. I reckon the fish in this creek would be full of vinegar, anyway. We're not a-staying where we're not wanted." She turned her back on the surly stranger.

Becky tried to forget the incident on the way to the campsite. She began asking about Oren and his father.

"What's your Pappy's name?"

"Jabe Storey."

"Haven't you got a mother?" she asked softly.

Oren shook his head. "My mother and sister died of the fever in March," he said. "And Pa's been having an awful time ever since. He just sat around just looking and staring, one week after another. He didn't plow our land or put in crops or take care of the stock. He didn't eat, hardly. I took care of things the best I could. It was only when somebody asked him to witch, he'd perk up."

"To witch? What's that?"

"Well-witch. You know, find water with a forked stick. Choose the right place to dig a well."

Becky shook her head. She had never heard of well-witching. They had a spring on their Ozark farm, bubbling into a rock-lined pool. They had never needed to dig for water. "Find water with a forked stick?" she exclaimed, unbelieving.

"With a branch of willow or peach wood, or almost any kind of green forked stick." There was quiet pride in Oren's voice. "Pa's got the feel for finding water. It's something not many people have. It's something between him and the earth, he says."

"What does he do with the stick?"

"Well, he holds it with one end of the fork in each hand and the stem up," Oren explained, going through the motions. "He holds it tight. Then he walks over the ground careful-like. When he gets above a water course, the stem points down real hard all of a sudden, so hard the stick almost jumps out of his hands sometimes. Pa can find where water is. He can even tell how deep to dig, 'most always."

Becky was impressed. "He must make a good living at that, finding water for people when they need it. He must make a lot of money."

Oren gave her a strange look. "Pa never charges for well-witching," he said slowly. "He says it's a gift the Lord gave him, a gift of being part of something big and wonderful nobody can understand. He wouldn't charge for a thing like that." For a moment Oren was silent. Then he went on. "That's why we haven't got much, Pa and me… after paying for the funeral, and him not working all summer, and hard times and all. That's why Pa thought he might get a fresh start out in the Race for the Prairie."

Becky liked Oren. He was different from the boys she knew back home. The boys her own age at school were always wrestling and fighting. This boy, you could talk to. You could learn things from him. And he felt things deep inside.

When they reached camp, the menfolk and Dave were near Sprinter, looking him over.

"Reckon he's just good as a saddle horse," Jabe Storey was saying. "Not much for pulling a rig."

"That's just where you're wrong," Becky's father answered quickly. "Sprinter can carry a rider or pull a rig. Either way he's fast. But of course he'll do best in the Run as a saddle horse, without pulling extra weight."

"Wish I had one like him," Jabe Storey sighed. "I won't

get much of a homestead, driving oxen."

"Why don't you leave your boy and the critters at Caldwell," Ross Fletcher asked, "and take the train into the Strip the day of the Run? I hear the Rock Island will be running special trains."

"I've been thinking of that, turning it over in my mind. I could take the train from Caldwell and jump off near Enid. They say Enid is bound to be one of the leading cities."

"You could jump off at any likely-looking place," Ross Fletcher continued. "I understand trains won't be allowed to go over fifteen miles an hour, so as not to outrun the horses."

"Sprinter can go faster than that, can't he, Pappy?" Dave asked.

"That he can," came the prompt answer. Turning to Mr. Storey again, he remarked, "Yes, I've heard that Enid is bound to become a city overnight. Queen city of the Race for the Prairie, they predict. But the better land is to the east, Storey. Costs a bit more, but I figure it's worth it. That's why I'm planning to make the Run from Arkansas City."

Before Jabe Storey could answer, Matt began to bang on a tin pie plate as he pranced around the fire. "Who's a-coming for supper? Who's a-coming to eat? Who's a-coming for cornbread, with sorghum on for sweet?"

"Where's the Promised Land?" Matt asked, when supper was over and they were sitting around the little campfire. "Where's it at?"

"'Tain't always the same place, son," Eliza Fletcher

answered. She was trying to patch overalls by firelight and the dancing flames made living bronze of her hair. "Not always the same piece of good earth. Now it's the Race for the Prairie. It was Old Oklahomy back in the spring of '89 when the first Indian Territory land was opened up."

Becky nodded. She had been no older then than Dave was now but she remembered how Granny had urged them to make the Run. She remembered the planning, the excitement, the rainbow hopes.

"We'll all go," her father had decided. "We'll get there in the spring, in time to plow the virgin soil for planting, and we'll make us a good home."

But three weeks before the Run that April, Granny broke her hip. She couldn't go along, and the folks wouldn't go without her. They had wanted to go when other lands in the Indian Territory were opened in 1891 and 1892. But always something happened.

Came the spring of 1893—this spring. The government paid the Cherokee Indians more than eight million dollars for the strip; and everyone knew the land would be opened to homesteaders within six months. The Fletchers must make the run this time or never! It would be the last big block of cheap land. They had to get themselves a good homestead. Well, Becky said to herself, here they were, on the way.

Her mother's voice rose and fell like the melody of a song. "The Promised Land, Matt? It's what Moses was a-searching for when he led the children of Israel across the Red Sea out of Egypt, hunting for the land of milk and honey."

"I reckon folks have always been looking for a Promised Land somewhere," Mr. Storey said. He was leaning toward the firelight, slowly and carefully whetting his jackknife on a hand stone. "There were the Pilgrims sailing across the stormy sea in the Mayflower, remember. And the '49ers rushing out to Californy. And the '59ers to Colorado. Seems folks are always out to find the Promised Land."

"But we're almost at the end of the road now," Becky said, abruptly. "We're heading for the last big piece of land the government has to open. There won't be any more big runs, will there, Pappy?"

Her father agreed. "No, there won't. This will be the biggest Run of all. If the Strip hadn't been kept apart for the Cherokees all these years, it would have been taken up long before now. Come September 16, it's our last chance for first-come, first-pick. And I'm counting on Sprinter and me being right up in front."

"I don't know what I'm counting on," Jabe Storey mumbled. "Except to get a fresh start in Oklahoma Territory."

"That's what thousands of folks are hoping," Becky's mother said, poking absent-mindedly at the dying fire. A shower of sparks rose up on bright, quick wings, and then flickered out.

"Well, I reckon it's time we turned in, folks. Tomorrow's another day for covering the miles."

"I'll be taking a last look at Sprinter and the mules," her husband said and strode off into the night.

Jabe Storey glanced up at the sky full of stars that

brightened the clear summer night. "Fine night for sleeping under the bright sky of Kansas, Oren," he said.

"Let's sleep out, too," Becky whispered to Matt. "There's a nice level spot there near the wagon, with a half a world of sky a-looping overhead. Get your blanket."

Soon the camp was quiet.

* * *

Becky didn't wake up with a start. She had a hard time opening her eyes, throwing off the clutch of sleep. But wasn't that a horse's neigh that had broken into her dream? Sprinter's? No, it was too far away, too dim and far away. Sprinter was tethered close and safe near the campground.

She half-opened her eyes. The moon was two hours high now, stealing light from the stars. Except for the jingle of katydids, all was still. She must have been dreaming to think she heard Sprinter neighing in the distance. Dreaming... In the moonlight she saw Oren sleeping near the Storeys' wagon. On the other side of Oren she saw another blanket crumpled on the grass.

She blinked and raised herself on her elbow. Mr. Storey's blanket was empty!

"He's probably just checking up on the oxen," Becky thought, "so they won't stray."

She lay down again and was drifting off to sleep when she heard a far-off shout. Then another.

This time Becky was fully awake, sitting up, looking

around. She tried to make out Sprinter's shape over in the grassy patch where he had been picketed. But there was no sign of Sprinter. He wasn't standing, and he didn't often lie down…

Alarmed, she threw off the corner of the blanket and headed for the picket pin. Where was Sprinter? Was his rope long enough for him to be lost in the shadows?

Becky reached the stake and picked up an end of rope. Sprinter was gone!

CHAPTER 2

Upsetting News

Becky stood there, holding the end of rope in her hand. This was not a case of Sprinter escaping. The rope had been cut. Sawed through with a sharp knife.

Suddenly she remembered how Jabe Storey had sat by the campfire carefully whetting his jackknife. Suspicious thoughts, like mosquitoes, began to buzz in her head. She tried to brush them off, but they kept buzzing. What did they know about Mr. Storey, anyway? Didn't Pappy say there would be sharpers aplenty trying to take advantage of folks making the Run? Hadn't he said the Fletchers would have to watch their step?

Though the night was pleasantly mild, Becky shivered as if she had a chill. Hadn't that boy said: "Wish we had a fast horse. Wish we could be in there at the front of the race." Jabe Storey, too, when he was looking Sprinter over: "Wish I had one like him."

Did Mr. Storey think he could make off with Sprinter when everyone was asleep? Hide him in the woods somewhere? And then go back and get him when the Fletchers gave up the hunt and moved on?

Becky turned back to the campsite. "No... no," something within her kept saying. "Yes... yes," something else persisted. "It would be an easy way to get a good horse." She moved softly over the dry Kansas grass.

Poking her head into the open flap of the tent, she whispered urgently, "Pappy! Pappy!"

"That you, Becky?" asked a sleepy voice.

"Pappy, Sprinter's gone."

"Gone!" In a second Ross Fletcher came out, carrying his boots. "What you a-saying, daughter?"

"Sprinter's gone. The rope's cut. And Jabe Storey is gone, too."

"What about the boy?"

"He's asleep, near his wagon." Becky found it hard to keep her voice down. "The rope's cut clean as a whistle, Pappy. I've been out there a-holding the end of it."

"And Storey's gone?"

"You don't think… you don't think he'd run off with the horse, do you?"

"I've not had time to think. Talk low, Becky, so's not to waken the folks."

Becky felt a little mean, but she had to say. "You saw Mr. Storey whetting his knife last night. And you heard him say he wished he had a horse like Sprinter. But he doesn't look like a horse thief, does he, Pappy?"

"You never can tell."

"You can, too!" Eliza Fletcher stood there in the opening of the tent. "I've been a-listening to what you two were whispering together. And, now, you listen to me. Mr.

Storey's no horse thief. Of that I'm sure, sure as a door turneth upon its hinges."

"How can you be so sure?" Becky asked.

Her mother turned and her face caught the quiet moonlight. She looked calm and confident. "Remember what you told me, Becky, when we were washing up after supper? About Mr. Storey being a well-witch and not charging for finding water? Feeling he was in touch with something big and wonderful he couldn't make money off'n? A man like that's no thief. He's not the kind to covet another man's horse."

"But there's evidence…" Ross Fletcher began lamely.

"The worst kind of evidence, Ross. Circumstantial evidence," his wife said quietly. "Look in your heart."

"What are we going to do?" Becky burst out. "Just sit and wait?"

Her mother answered calmly. "Mr. Storey will be back. His boy's here, and his wagon's here, and his critters are here. He'll be back and have his own words to speak."

"Reckon there's nothing to do but wait," Ross Fletcher said. "We wouldn't know where to start looking, anyway."

"But don't be harboring thoughts like thorns and thistles while you're a-waiting," his wife warned. "Don't be judging by circumstantial evidence." Her words lingered in the air as she disappeared in the tent.

Becky and her father moved toward the dead embers of the campfire, where Pappy had just put the wagon seat. "Shall we have ourselves a fire?" Becky asked.

"We'd best just be sitting in the moonlight when Jabe Storey comes back, wherever he's gone. As for Sprinter, I don't know what to say. Wonder what time it is. Must have left my watch a-hanging on the tent pole." He slipped back to get it.

Becky saw the flicker of a match when her father returned. "What time is it, Pappy?"

"Past one o'clock in the morning."

They sat there next to each other on the wagon seat without talking. Becky had never felt more wide awake. Above the sound of the katydids, she could hear the oxen nearby, chewing their cuds. The tethered mules stomped and fidgeted. Time was a shadow that stretched behind the wagons, the tent and every clump of weeds. Matt and that Storey boy kept sleeping.

"Katydid, she didn't, she did," suddenly began to sound to Becky like "Storey did, he didn't, he did." How were they going to find out? How were they going to get Sprinter back? And without Sprinter, how would they ever be able to make the Run into the Strip?

Suddenly there came the sound of hoofs on the road, way off to the east. It was a late hour for anyone to be traveling.

"That a horse?" her father asked. "You hear a horse, Becky?"

They waited, straining their ears. It was a horse, all right, coming closer, trotting down the road.

The hoof beats sounded louder. As they neared the campsite, the horse slowed down to a walk. Becky turned to her father questioningly.

"Best just sit and wait, daughter."

They could see the dark shape of horse and rider now, turning off the road toward the silent wagons. Then the rider slipped down and began leading the horse toward the picket stake. Becky clutched her father's arm. It was Sprinter! No other horse held his head just like that, proud and high. You could tell even in the moonlight. It was Sprinter!

With a nod of his head Ross Fletcher stood up and started forward. Becky followed. They walked quietly toward Sprinter. The figure bending over the broken rope looked like Oren's father.

"Hello, there. That you, Storey?"

Mr. Storey turned around, startled. "Oh! You up? Fine night for exercising a horse wouldn't you say?" Becky imagined she could hear a chuckle in the words.

"Reckon it is," her father said quietly.

"Your horse got some good night exercise he wasn't counting on," Jabe Storey remarked.

"But you... nobody had to cut the rope for that," Becky said in a voice that couldn't keep from trembling. "It could have been untied at the stake, easy-like."

"Reckon somebody wanted a piece of rope to lead the horse away with."

Becky's thoughts were in a turmoil. If Mr. Storey led Sprinter away, why did he bring him back? Did he decide he didn't want to hide him in the woods, after all?

"What happened?" Becky's father asked.

The tale was told in Jabe Storey's low, patient drawl. Standing there near the shadows, rubbing the white streak on Sprinter's nose, Becky listened.

"Ever since my wife died in the spring," Mr. Storey began, "I've been sleeping light as a cat. It was the same tonight. I was lying there listening to the night noises, watching the stars inch along the sky, knowing the rest of you were asleep... and that I ought to be. Then, all of a sudden, I heard unusual sounds from Sprinter's direction. Heard him stomping. Heard a muffled neigh.

"I got up to see what was wrong, walking over in my bare feet, keeping stealthy-quiet so as not to wake you all. And I reached the picket pin just in time to see a man leading Sprinter away in the direction of the woods along the creek. I lost time having to run back for my shoes," he explained, "but I knew I'd need them, trying to follow a horse thief across country."

Ross Fletcher nodded.

"By the time I caught sight of Sprinter again, the man was leading him through a little clearing near the creek. I couldn't figure what to do. Didn't know if the man was armed or not. Didn't think I'd be much good standing up singlehanded to a horse thief with a gun."

"So what did you do?" Becky whispered.

"I figured I had to take advantage of that clearing," Jabe Storey went on. "So I yelled out good and loud: 'There he is, Amos! You can get a good shot at him now. Close in, Johnny! Don't let the thief get away. Block him in the woods, Fred. Mind you don't hit the horse by mistake.'"

Jabe chuckled out loud. "I kept whacking two sticks together and shouting like I had a whole army with me. You never saw a guilty man drop a rope so fast in your life. You never saw a man skedaddle so quick. 'Give it to him, Amos,' I yelled. And then I ran up and grabbed Sprinter's rope.

"The rest was easy. I led Sprinter out to where I thought the road should be, and came riding him back to camp in the moonlight." Jabe laughed, enjoying the incident now that it was over. "Fine night for exercising a horse."

"What kind of man was the thief?" Becky asked. "Real tall and lanky?" She had a suspicion she knew who it was.

"Tall with a stoop to the shoulders."

"That's the man heard me telling Oren about Sprinter when we were at the creek! That's the man warned us to get off his property!"

"I'm beholden to you, Storey, for rescuing the horse," her father said simply.

"Beholden, nothing. It was a real pleasure, I tell you, to be staying awake, once, for some good." Mr. Storey gave a pat on the thigh. "You won't have to worry about the horse anymore tonight, I reckon."

Ross Fletcher laughed. "Reckon we won't. Not with Amos and Johnny and Fred a-waiting to take a bead on the horse thief!"

Next morning at breakfast all they talked about was Sprinter, and the horse thief and Jabe Storey. "'Twasn't nothing," Jabe kept saying, modest-like. "Nothing at all."

Becky didn't say much. She had a strange feeling inside. It kept pricking at her like a thorn. She had begrudged having her mother open the best jar of blackberry preserves for the Storeys last night! And she'd thought Jabe Storey might steal a horse just because he wanted one! Becky passed her hand over the pocket where she kept her gold cartridge pencil. It made a worn place where it rubbed against her petticoat. For the first time the pencil didn't seem so precious… considering how she had got it. Considering what she had done when she wanted something real bad.

"I reckon we won't be seeing you folks again," Jabe Storey was saying. "You'll be moving along twenty-five, thirty miles a day with the mules. We'll only be doing about fifteen with the oxen."

"We might see them when we go through Arkansas City, Pa!" Oren said hopefully.

Becky said nothing but she was hopeful, too. She'd give a lot to see Oren again.

"Only one chance in a thousand, son," Oren's father said, shaking his head. "There'll be a crowd already gathered there for the Run, when we drive through Arkansas City. It would be like looking for a needle in a haystack… or a pitchfork, anyway. Well…" He held out his hand to all the Fletchers in turn, beginning with Becky's mother. "It's been a real pleasure to camp with you folks. And I commend your cooking, Mrs. Fletcher. I'm wishing you all the best of luck on the Run. Hope you get yourselves a special-fine homestead."

"You, too," Eliza Fletcher answered.

When he came to Becky, Mr. Storey winked and said, "Don't forget to exercise that horse!"

***

They were on the road again, the dusty Kansas road, heading for the Promised Land. It was mid-afternoon. Becky's mother was driving the mules, with Dave taking his turn beside her on the wagon seat. Pappy was up ahead on the road, giving Sprinter a workout. Becky and Matt were walking behind the wagon to get the kinks out of their legs.

"Will there be lots of cherry trees, Becky?" Matt asked. "With cherries on?"

"What do you mean? Where?"

"When we get to the strip of cherry trees."

Becky looked at her little brother. She never could tell when Matt was fooling. She could never make up her mind if he was dumb as an oyster or smart as a whip. Matt had a way of keeping his face so innocent-like.

"Never heard tell of a strip of cherry trees," Becky said.

"You did, too. Everybody has. It's where we're going… to the Cherry Tree Strip."

"Oh, the Race for the Prairie."

"That's what I said. I'm glad we're going to live in a place with such a pretty name, aren't you, Becky?"

***

Hot, tired and dusty, the Fletchers reached Arkansas City on the afternoon of September seventh. Now the Ozarks seemed a world away, and the Promised Land almost underfoot. Becky spotted the big A. C. Flour Mill and the Santa Fe Railroad tracks as they approached the busy town. And Dave pointed out the high buildings in the business district.

Although the Run was still nine days away, Arkansas City was like a river at flood tide, flowing over. The place was jammed with horses and wagons of all descriptions, and people—people gathering to make the race for a homestead.

"Why do they call it Arkansas City, Becky?" Matt wanted to know. "When it's not in Arkansas at all, but in Kansas?"

"I don't know." How did Matt think of all those questions?

"Why, Ma?"

"Well, I reckon 'cause it's sitting on the bank of the Arkansas River, child. And that's an important river for a city to be sitting on."

Becky was next to her mother on the wagon seat as they pulled into town. She had pushed back her sunbonnet so she wouldn't miss a thing. The boys hung over the seat and Pappy trotted close to the wagon on Sprinter.

"Mercy, I haven't laid eyes on so many people in years," Eliza Fletcher called to her husband. "It kind of scares me, Ross. A country woman like me."

"Looks as if it's going to be the First Run all over again, Eliza. More people gathered at Arkansas City four years ago than at any other place. Looks as if it's going to be that-a-way again."

"They had to race farther that time, didn't they?" Becky asked. "To old Oklahomy?"

"Lots farther. Coming from the north, they had to race clear through the Race for the Prairie—that's fifty-eight miles alone. Clear through to the heart of the Indian Territory."

Mrs. Fletcher pulled back on the reins just in time to avoid locking wheels with a wagon backing out from a hitching post. They were driving down Summit Street, and it was crowded.

"Look," cried Dave. "Look what's printed on that covered wagon. TO THE PROMISED LAND. That's where we're going, isn't it?"

"At this rate there'll be a line a mile long to register for the Run, when the government booth opens on Monday," Pappy shouted, drawing close to the wagon again. "Reckon I'll have to stand in line with the rest, a-waiting my turn."

His wife turned toward him quickly, tender-like. "I dread to think of it, Ross. You standing in line for hours in the hot sun, after that sunstroke you had two years ago. I dread to think of it. Couldn't we go somewhere else, where it wouldn't be so crowded? Didn't you say there'd be nine booths around the Strip? Nine places a person could register?"

Her husband nodded. "But the best land's on this side, south of Arkansas City, Eliza. I'd not let a little thing like standing in the sun change my mind. No, sir."

Becky knew that was true. It would take more than "a little thing" to make her father change his mind.

"Oh, look at that funny covered wagon," Matt exclaimed. "What does the writing say?"

Dave grinned. Then slowly he read aloud: CINCH BUGGED IN ILLINOIS, SICLONED IN NEBRASKA, OKLAHOMA OR BUST.

"Most of these folks are from Kansas and Arkansas, I reckon," their mother said. "And Missouri. But they'll be here from all over the country, a-trying to get themselves a piece of land. There's a mighty strong hunger in folks for land. Always has been, and always will be."

They finally found a camping place on the south side of town not far from the river. Other home-seekers were camped nearby. Ross Fletcher pushed back his old straw hat that showed a stain around the hatband. "Over there," he said, pointing south, "is the Promised Land. We're only about four miles from the border."

Becky stared. She didn't know what she had expected, but the rolling farmland ahead didn't look any different from the dry country they had been driving through since reaching Kansas.

"You sit in the shade and rest a mite, Eliza," Ross Fletcher suggested. "You and the young 'uns. Becky can take a turn with me through town. A-keeping our ears open, mayhap we can pick up some talk about the Run. Want to come, daughter?"

"Wait till I put on my shoes," Becky said. Always, since she was small, she'd been going on exploring trips with her father—only now it wasn't up the creek or over the fields, but in a city. She'd have to wear shoes.

Reaching Summit Street, they made their way slowly along the crowded boardwalk. In front of the hotel, men were talking in little groups. "There'll be thirty thousand people starting the race from here," Becky heard one man say as they passed. "I'm taking bets on it. What do you say, Mister?" The man grasped Ross Fletcher's arm. "Want to make a bet?"

"No, thanks," he answered hastily.

"Thirty thousand people!" Becky gasped. Would thirty thousand people really try to crowd into the Strip from one place? How could thirty thousand people register at one booth in a week's time?

"That's a lot of folks," her father agreed. For the first time there was anxiety in his voice. "If it's going to be that-a-way, Becky, there won't be near enough homesteads to go around. I read in the paper the government was expecting only about fifty thousand in all to make the run. But with thirty thousand going in from Arkansas City alone, there'll be a good hundred thousand a-wanting in from all four sides." He shook his head. "It'll be a stiff race. A lot stiffer than I counted on."

"Don't forget we've got Sprinter, Pappy."

"That's right, we've got Sprinter. He'll have to find us a homestead no matter how many folks are making the Run."

A cheer went up as a thoroughbred racehorse came trotting down the street, lifting his slender legs delicately as if trying to avoid the dust. Becky and her father stopped to watch. The thoroughbred seemed nervous, shying away from horses and wagons, tossing his head. He was sleek, well-bred in every muscle.

"That's a beautiful piece of horseflesh," Becky's father remarked. "Sleek, well-bred."

The man standing next to him turned. He wore the broad-brimmed hat and tight-fitting shirt of a cowman, and high-heeled boots.

"A beautiful piece of horseflesh, but what's he good for?" the man demanded.

"Why, put him in a race, a horse like that will come out in front," Ross Fletcher answered.

"What kind of race, Mister? You talking about the county fair?"

"Well, yes. That horse would do fine on the track at a county fair."

"All right, if that's what you mean, I agree with you. But the biggest horse race in the world is going to take place in these parts a week from Saturday. And it's not going to be run on any race track. It's going to be run across the virgin sod of the prairie, where the going is rough, where prairie-dog holes are waiting to catch a horse's hoof. There'll be gullies to cross, and streams with quicksand in them…"

Becky felt her cheeks turning red. She couldn't help comparing Sprinter to that bronze-colored thoroughbred. Sprinter had just such slender neck and legs. The Fletchers hadn't thought about the rough kind of racing it would be!

"When it comes to the Run next week," the stranger went on, "I wouldn't take ten thoroughbreds like that for one sturdy little cow pony. Give me a horse with wide shoulders and a deep chest and strong legs to make the race into the Race for the Prairie. Give me a horse that's used to being ridden over rough prairie mile after mile."

"I hadn't thought of it like that," Ross Fletcher muttered.

"Most folks don't," the stranger said. "That's why you're going to see the wildest lot of horseflesh and rigs ever gathered together in the history of the world. Mark my words."

Becky could see that her father was worried, as he asked, "What would you do, sir… if you had to get a homestead, but didn't own a cow pony?"

"What if you had a real good track-running horse instead?" Becky put in anxiously. "Not a thoroughbred, but real good?"

The stranger turned to look at her, then back to her father. "Your horse had any experience running across open country?"

Ross Fletcher shook his head. Old Brant had been interested only in racetracks. Sprinter was a track-trained horse.

"Well, I'll tell you. If I were in your place, I wouldn't

make the run from Arkansas City. I'd rather take my chance from Caldwell. The Chisholm Trail—greatest old cattle trail in the world—ran through Caldwell on its way from San Antonio to Abilene. It hasn't been used much since the railroads came in and the big cattle drives stopped. But the trail's still tramped down from the millions and millions of cow hoofs that passed over it in the '60s."

"The Chisholm Trail," Becky's father repeated. "I've heard tell of it."

"Mind, I'm not saying it's a fancy road," the stranger hastened to add. "But it's a couple hundred yards wide most places, and considerably better than raw prairie. More cows have beaten it down than any other trail in the world. And it's the only road into the Strip."

"A man could ride into the Strip on the Old Chisholm Trail?"

The cowman nodded. "Better than over virgin prairie. And the land's right good south of Caldwell, in and around the townsite the government has picked at Enid. And only $1.50 an acre. There's to be a land office at Enid, you know. A man wouldn't have to go far to file on his land if he staked near there. I'm thinking I might make the Run from Caldwell myself, just for the sport of it."

Enid. That was the townsite Oren and his father had talked about. Becky caught at a hope. If only the Fletchers and Storeys could get homesteads near each other, they wouldn't be strangers in a strange land. If only…

"I'm obliged to you for the information," her father said.

"I'm a new hand at this kind of horse racing. Much obliged to you, stranger."

"Always glad to put in a good word for a cow pony," the cowman said good-naturedly.

Becky and her father turned back toward camp. "I can see the sense of it," Ross Fletcher said. "Can't figure out why I never thought of it myself. Sprinter might do well enough at the start, but he's not used to rough sod underfoot."

"Or running over prairie-dog holes."

"Sprinter would get winded right quick, I'm afeared. Might even stumble in a gully and break a leg."

"No, Pappy!"

"Couldn't be sure he wouldn't, Becky. He's not trained for rough going like that."

They tramped through the dust toward camp. But Becky didn't notice how dusty and dry and hot the afternoon was. After all their pride in Sprinter, all their talk of getting one of the best homesteads in the Promised Land, all their hopes and dreams… here they were, a-wondering what to do!

"Reckon we'd best talk it over with your mother this evening," her father said as they neared camp. "Look at it top and bottom."

"I reckon so, Pappy." Becky tried to sound cheerful, but her voice trembled. Getting a homestead wasn't going to be so easy after all, even with a horse like Sprinter. Becky was scared, plumb scared.

CHAPTER 3

Bad Luck at Caldwell

There was nothing to do, the Fletchers decided, but go on to Caldwell. They had to get a homestead, and it was best to go where Sprinter could make a safe run. Becky was glad. Caldwell was the place the Storeys were heading for. They might even get homesteads not too far apart!

Mid-morning on the 9th of September, just a week before the Run, the Fletchers reached the Chikaskia River, near Caldwell. The water was low after the heat and dryness of summer but at least it was water.

"Best stop and give Sprinter and the mules a good drink," Ross Fletcher said. "And fill our kegs and containers. Chances are water will be scarce in Caldwell, with land seekers a-gathering there by the hundred."

Containers full and stock watered, the Fletchers drove on to Caldwell. The little cowtown appealed to them all much more than big, bustling Arkansas City. But even Caldwell was mushrooming. Tents and covered wagons dotted the prairie on the outskirts of town, especially to the south—toward the border of the Race for the Prairie. Horses and wagons were everywhere.

"Seems you're still a-going to have to stand in line to register, Ross," Becky's mother remarked, as they looked around for a good camping place.

"I didn't expect to see so many folks a-gathered here," her husband admitted. "May turn out to be half as many as at Arkansas City. I reckon it's the Chisholm Trail attracts them. The way it beckons us."

"I'd be glad to register for you, if I could, Ross. It won't do for you to be getting another sunstroke."

He grinned. "Register for me? You're over twenty-one, right enough, Eliza. But I reckon you're not the head of the family in the eyes of the law, howsoever it seems in the eyes of the rest of us!"

"Go along with you," Eliza Fletcher flashed back. "You know well enough who's head of the family, Ross, whatever way you look at it!"

"I don't see why you have to stand in line, anyway, Pappy," Becky put in. "Homesteaders didn't have to register before, you said. Not in the run of '89."

"They didn't have to pay for the land then, either. Now we pay for every acre. We still have to live on the land five years, and make improvements, same as before."

They were unpacking the wagon now, putting up the tent, making themselves at home. They had found a good campsite south of town, not far from other campers.

"I'm in favor of registration," Becky's father said. With great care he was easing Granny's rocking chair out of the back of the wagon. "Registration aims to keep out the Sooners. It's to prevent folks from slipping over the border ahead of time, the way they did in '89."

Sooners. They were the ones who wouldn't wait to take their chance fair and square with the other settlers. They were the ones who slipped across the border before the land was opened. When Old Oklahoma was opened in 1889, Sooners hid themselves in ravines along a creek and staked out claims before honest homesteaders had a chance to get there.

Becky had heard how Sooners dashed out of hiding the day of the opening, and made believe they'd taken part in the Run. Some of them even threw water over their horses and rubbed them with soap, so they looked as if they had galloped themselves into a lather... in case an officer happened around.

Sooners didn't play fair. Of course, if they were caught, they couldn't get title to their homesteads. But many had tricked the law in the first big Run.

"I say anything to stop Sooners is to the good," Pappy was saying. "If registration will do it, I'm for standing in line till I drop. Me, I don't want any truck with Sooners. Most of them never intend to prove up their claims, but they'll threaten an honest homesteader with trouble till they get a hundred dollars out of him, or a good horse, or some such."

Eliza Fletcher was busy making the camp a homey place. After all, the family would be camping near Caldwell for more than a week, until her husband got back from riding Sprinter in the Run, and filing his claim at the Enid land office. Then they would break camp for the last time and head for their new home in the Race for the Prairie.

"When we get to the homestead, Pappy, we can lift off the wagon box, with the canvas top still on," Becky said. "Between that and the tent we'll get along all right till we can build a house."

"Till we build ourselves a dwelling of the virgin sod," Ross Fletcher boomed, with a dramatic gesture. "We'll lay up sod, and make our walls so thick." He measured off a good two feet with his hands. "Keep out the sun in summer and the winter cold. And we'll just be out of pocket for the windows and doors, that's all."

"And whitewash, Ross," his wife said. "You promised me you'd whitewash all the inside walls."

"So I did, Eliza. Well, five dollars, six dollars ought to take care of the store expense for a two-room sod house on our chosen site."

"A soddy house like a prairie mouse!" Matt sang out, as he dashed about helping the chickens catch grasshoppers.

Becky was listening, with the old dreamy look in her eyes. Absent-mindedly, she put down the bedding she was carrying to the tent.

"You thinking about our house too, Becky?" her father asked.

Becky's rainbow had a house in it, all right. But it wasn't a sod house looking like a hump in the prairie. "I'm thinking of a big frame house painted green and white," she answered slowly. "With shingles on the roof, and a fancy porch with doodads on. After we get the harvest in, I mean."

Her mother was beginning to fry mush over a little fire.

She looked up. "Takes more than one harvest for a house like that, daughter. But it's a dream to harbor."

After the noon meal Ross Fletcher was anxious to ride Sprinter down the old Chisholm Trail to the border of the Strip. It was only about four miles south of Caldwell, he said, and Sprinter needed a fast workout. He was anxious to find out what the Trail was like; and was curious, besides, to see how well the line was guarded. Could they really keep the Sooners out this time?

"Before you go, Ross," his wife said, "give Becky a dime, will you? We're a-running short of sal soda, and she can walk to town for a good supply."

Becky put on her shoes and her best skirt and her sunbonnet. She was glad for a chance to mingle with the noisy crowd that filled Caldwell's main street. It was more like the 4th of July than the 9th of September. She bought the bag of soda first and then walked along the street, eyes and ears open.

When would Oren and his father get here with their ox team? Not until Tuesday or Wednesday, probably. And when they did come, would the Storeys and the Fletchers meet in all this crowd? She wished Oren were here now, walking beside her. Then she wouldn't feel like such a stranger, with strangers all around.

A group of men were standing in front of the boarding house, talking loudly. Becky slowed her pace to listen.

"Register! Bosh. Nothing but a big joke."

"It's Uncle Sam's notion of how to keep the Sooners out, ain't you heard?"

"How, I'd like to know?"

"If folks have to register, they won't have so much chance to find an unguarded place on the border where they can slip in."

"It may keep out a few. I don't know."

"What's to prevent a Sooner from registering early in the week? That would give him three, four days to find a way into the Strip when the soldiers weren't looking. And he'd have his registration certificate, to present at the land office, like anyone else."

"That's right."

"Let me tell you… it will take more than a registration booth to stop a Sooner."

Slowly, thoughtfully, Becky moved down the street. Was Pappy wrong about registration keeping out Sooners? Everyone knew there weren't nearly enough soldiers to guard the Strip. More than four hundred miles of border would take a whole army of soldiers! If a man wanted to be dishonest, why couldn't he register early and find some way to slip in ahead of the others? Maybe Pappy was just too honest himself to imagine the scheming ways of others. Just too honest…

Becky's fingers closed around the cartridge pencil in her pocket. A little chill ran through her. She had been feeling more and more uncomfortable about that pencil lately. The way Granny said she would.

"You look on it as a prized possession now, Becky," she'd said, guessing in her shrewd way, how her granddaughter got the pencil. "But it's the kind of gold that tarnishes."

Becky flushed under her sunbonnet. Suddenly she wasn't in the strange noisy street of Caldwell, Kansas, anymore. She was back in the Ozarks, coming home that mild July evening, flourishing the pencil...

"Look what Old Brant gave me for the beans I picked and the berries I sold him!"

"'Stead of the dollar?" Pappy asked.

"It's worth more than a dollar, Pappy."

"I was counting on the dollar toward the mortgage interest, Becky." He took the pencil and examined it, pulling out the red-writing end, then the blue-writing end. "That's a tricky pencil, and there's gold in the metal, I reckon. It's no doubt worth more than a dollar. But it won't help to pay the interest."

"Where did Old Brant get a pencil like that?" Becky's mother wanted to know.

"Swapping horses. He got it thrown in on a deal."

"And he made you take it, 'stead of your pay," Ross Fletcher accused. "That's like Old Brant. Anything to save himself a dollar. He's getting work out of you cheap enough." He turned away, and never said another word about the pencil.

But Granny did. "What'd you do it for, Becky?" she had asked that very night when they were alone, sitting at the kitchen table after the others had gone to bed.

"Do what, Gran?" Becky's face grew red.

"That wasn't the whole truth about the pencil. I knew from the look of you."

Becky defended herself. "I never had anything all my own like that before. Never in my life. I never had anything fine and boughten like that pencil. Look, Granny..." She showed how it worked and turned it in the light of the kerosene lamp so the gold gleamed and glittered.

"It's a fancy-bright pencil, right enough," Granny admitted. "But it'll tarnish, Becky...considering you could have had the dollar to give to your father." She fixed her flax-blue eyes upon her granddaughter. "You could have had the dollar, couldn't you, Becky?"

"Yes-s-s." Becky confessed, the way she always confessed to Gran. "Old Brant would have given me the dollar. He had it ready. He had it in his hand. But all I could think of was the pencil, ever since the time he showed it to me. So I asked to see it again."

"And Old Brant said it would be a fine pencil for a bright girl like you to have?"

Becky nodded. "Said it was something I could keep for my own forever. Something I wouldn't have to turn over to my family like money. Said if I didn't look out for myself, nobody else would. Said more things like that."

"He said you were old enough to have a pencil like that if you wanted one, didn't he?"

Then Gran said something about the secret of happiness not being in things. Becky couldn't remember the exact words. She'd pushed them out of her mind then, and she'd kept pushing them out ever since.

'Course, it hadn't been fair to Pappy. Children were supposed to turn over their earnings when they were living at home, and the family was fighting a mortgage together. And so little cash money coming in...

Suddenly Becky was jolted out of the past right back to the dusty street of Caldwell. "Get your map of the Race for the Prairie!" a hawker nearby was shouting. "Complete map of the Strip. Best map on the market today." Standing beside a dry-goods box in front of a store, stood a man waving a map. Copies were piled on the box beside him. "Here's your guide to the Promised Land, folks. First-rate map of the Strip, showing the sites of the four government land offices–Perry, Enid, Alva, and Woodward. Showing the seven townsites. To say nothing of the creeks and hollows, and even the prairie-dog holes! Only a dollar. Only a dollar for the best little map on the market."

Two farmers stopped and bought maps. A woman in a checked gingham dress stepped up. "Does it show the Chisholm Trail?"

"Sure does, Lady. Shows the Trail running south from Caldwell, clear through the Strip."

"Has it got the Salt Fork on?"

"The Salt Fork branch of the Arkansas River? Well, I should say."

"Then I'll take one," the woman said, handing over a silver dollar.

Becky stood on the edge of the crowd, watching. It would be a fine thing to get hold of a map like that. Then Pappy would know what to head for when he raced down the Chisholm Trail the day of the opening!

"Your best chance to pick a choice homestead is to

have a map," the salesman shouted. "Step up, ladies and gentlemen, for a true, authentic map of the Promised Land."

Becky edged closer. The fingers of her hand closed around the pencil in her skirt pocket. She didn't have a dollar. But she had something else.

The hawker spotted her. "You hankering for a map, Miss?"

"Yes, sir."

"Only costs a dollar. Planning to make the Run?"

"Not me. My father."

"Figured you looked a little young for twenty-one," the man said. "Or head of a family, either."

"Would you… consider making a swap, sir?" Becky asked.

"What you got to swap?"

"Something worth more than a dollar."

"Now don't tell me it's a jackknife! I've already swapped for three jackknives today."

Becky took out the pencil. It gleamed in the sunlight. "There's gold in it," she said and proudly showed how it worked.

"Quite a pencil! Where'd you get it? You're sure it's yours to swap?"

Becky flushed. "I worked for it—picking beans and berries, back in Missouri."

The man took the pencil and examined it carefully, up

and down and inside. "I'm willing to swap you a map for it," he said finally. "Here you are."

Clutching the true, authentic map of the Promised Land, Becky hurried home.

Before she reached the tents she knew that her father was back from his ride to the border. There was Sprinter, tethered safe to the wagon wheel. Good old Sprinter!

Matt came running to meet her. "Pappy saw soldiers on horseback stretched all along the border," he called. "And I found out what it means."

"What does it mean?"

"Two different things, depending on who you ask."

"What are you talking about, Matt? The soldiers mean only one thing—that nobody's allowed to go into the Race for the Prairie until 12 o'clock noon, next Saturday."

"I wasn't a-talking about the soldiers, Becky. But about Oklahomy. Don't you want to know?"

Before Becky had time to say she had more important things on her mind, Matt rattled on. "I asked five different people in camp and no one knew what Oklahomy meant. Then I saw a man wearing glasses, going around selling maps…"

"Maps!" Becky gasped. "Did Pappy buy one, Matt? Did he buy one?"

"Oh, no. Pappy wasn't home yet and Mama wouldn't pay a whole dollar for a map without asking him."

Becky sighed with relief, but Matt didn't notice. "So I asked the map man what it meant and he said Oklahoma is an Indian word that means Land of the Red Man."

"Then that's settled," Becky said, hurrying ahead. She was eager to show Pappy the map.

"No, it isn't settled, either. Because I asked a real smart lady and she said Oklahoma was the Indian word for Beautiful Land. So what am I going to believe, Becky?"

"That's easy. Put the two of them together. Then you'll have Beautiful Land of the Red Man. You couldn't be a-wanting anything better than that."

***

Ross Fletcher was telling his wife about the Chisholm Trail. He was sitting in front of the tent, with his lap full of harness that needed mending. Mrs. Fletcher was rocking in Gran's chair. "It's no fancy highway, Eliza. But you can still see how it's tramped down by the millions of cows that passed over it. And it's good and wide. Sprinter should do right well on the Chisholm Trail, if I only knew where to turn off for a good homestead."

"There was a map man around this morning, Ross," his wife said.

"There was? Reckon we ought to have a map, 'stead of stabbing around in the dark."

"But a dollar ... do you think it would be worth a whole dollar, Ross—a whole dollar?"

"Might be worth a good sight more than a dollar, Eliza."

"Oh, I hope so," Becky broke in. She held out the map.

"Then I'd be paying you some interest on that dollar you never got, Pappy."

"What you a-talking about, daughter? What dollar?"

Becky took off her sunbonnet and shook back her hair. It wasn't easy to begin but, once started, she poured out the whole tale—about the pencil and Gran. And how mean she felt about accusing Jabe Storey.

Everything was all pretty mixed up, but it must have made sense, because when she finished, her father said, simple-like, "Your slate's clean as a whistle now, Becky. And I don't know anything I'd rather have with that dollar than a map of the Race for the Prairie."

***

Late in the afternoon Becky and her father went to town together, to pick up any news that might be making the rounds.

For one thing they learned that not everyone crowding into the Kansas border town was expecting to make the Run. Many had just come out of curiosity, to see the big show, to watch the greatest race in the world. At that, people were saying that at least a hundred thousand home-seekers would be tearing into the Strip from all sides when the guns went off.

"How's your arithmetic, Becky?" her father asked. "How does six and a half million acres, in round numbers, divide up among a hundred thousand homesteaders?"

In school Becky had been good at arithmetic. Quickly, in her mind, she knocked off five zeros from each figure. That left 65 divided by 1. "Sixty-five acres for each homesteader, Pappy. But that can't be right."

"No?"

"A homesteader is entitled to 160 acres."

Her father nodded grimly. "If he gets there in time, he is. If he gets there first. 'Course, some of the folks will be seeking lots in the townsites the government had laid out. Town-folk are entitled to one lot each. But that will still leave twice as many folks a-seeking quarter sections as there will be quarter sections to go around."

"You mean half of the homesteaders are going to get left out, Pappy?"

"Looks like it, Becky. We've just got to see to it we aren't among them."

They stopped to watch a prairie schooner grind by. Its top was cluttered with writing, IN GOD WE TRUSTED AND IN COLORADO BUSTED. LET HER RIP: WE'RE GOING TO THE Race for the Prairie.

Ross Fletcher read the words aloud and chuckled. "That's what I say, daughter. Let her rip. Sprinter and I will be racing to the Race for the Prairie!"

There was sudden commotion ahead on the street, shouting and yelling. Passersby turned and ran for the shelter of buildings. "Something seems to be ripping right now," Becky's father muttered. Instead of turning back, he hurried ahead. "Watch out!" he cried.

Louder shouts and terrified screams came down the

street. "Whoa! Whoa, there."

"Look out for the steers!"

"Watch those longhorns! Run for your life!"

Then, through the cloud of churned-up dust, Becky saw what the commotion was. A bunch of longhorn steers came rampaging down the street. They were kicking up the dust, scaring horses and people.

Nearby, a horse hitched to a fancy buckboard was rearing on its hind legs. Becky could see a frightened young man on the seat sawing at the horse's mouth with the reins. The young woman beside him was white and terrified. The rig tipped. Another lunge like that would turn it over…

Now someone was running in front of the bucking horse. A man jumped and grasped the bridle. Becky gasped when she saw the man was her father. Pappy trying to keep the horse from bolting! Trying to stop a runaway! She clenched her teeth and waited.

Then, to her horror, she saw the horse lunge forward and knock her father to the road, knock him good and hard. In a moment he was up again, grasping the bridle with his other hand but blood was running down his face where the horse's hoof had struck his head.

The driver of the rig leapt out to help hold the frightened horse. The steers were out of sight, thundering down toward the railway stock pens. The shouting died down. The runaway had been stopped.

"How'd those steers get loose?" Becky heard a man behind her ask.

"I wouldn't put it past one of the cattlemen doing it a-purpose," came the answer. "They've no love for homesteaders. Ever since the government bought the Strip and ordered all cattle out, cattlemen have been sore."

"That's right."

"They're sore because they can't keep renting cheap pasture from the Cherokees. The Strip will soon be all fenced off into farms."

"Letting steers rampage down a busy street like that!" another voice exclaimed. "Somebody might have been killed."

Becky, pressing forward, saw her father pass his left hand over his head. The other arm dangled in a strange way, as if all the life had gone out of it.

"I'm a-coming, Pappy," she cried. But before she could reach him, her father slumped to the ground.

CHAPTER 4

Becky Gets an Idea

"Where's a doctor? Somebody get a doctor! There's a man hurt here." The young man holding the horse appealed to the crowd collecting around the buckboard.

Becky, kneeling at her father's side, looked up. "It's my father. Can somebody help?"

A man in a light-colored suit pressed through the bystanders. "What's wrong here? I'm a doctor. Step back folks. Give him some air."

"He stopped my runaway horse," the driver of the buckboard said. "We could have been killed, my wife and I. He grabbed the bridle just in time. Take care of him doctor and I'll foot the bill. I'm to blame for it all."

"Keep the crowd back," the doctor ordered. He turned to a husky-looking cowboy. "Keep them back, will you?" Then he bent over Ross Fletcher.

Becky saw her father open his eyes. "My arm," he mumbled. "Got me in the arm."

"Yes, that's right," the doctor said. "Compound fracture of the right arm. Bad cut in the head, too. Do you think you can walk?"

"I reckon so. I'm still a little dizzy-like."

"Here, lean on me," the doctor said. "Take it easy. Stand back, folks. Keep away from that broken arm! All right, sir. It won't be far to walk to the hotel."

"I'll be with you as soon as I get the horse to the livery stable," the owner of the buckboard said. "My name's Bowman, Henry Bowman." He turned to his wife. "Wait for me at the hotel, Lettie."

"I'm here, Pappy," Becky kept saying, as she walked beside the strange procession heading for the hotel. "Want I should go tell Mama?"

"Not yet, daughter. Not till we hear what the Doc says." Becky's father managed a weak smile. "Guess I'll live through it."

Live through it! Of course, you'll live through it, Becky thought. Her father's calm voice had swept away her panic. Then her mind leapt ahead to the race for the homestead. Would Pappy be able to ride Sprinter in the race, with a fractured arm?

"I'm new here," the doctor said, as they walked slowly toward the two-story frame hotel. "Name's Dowell. Dr. Charles Dowell, from Kansas City. I figured the new townsite of Enid would be a good place to set up a practice."

"Looks as if some folks need a doctor before the Strip opens," Ross Fletcher remarked grimly.

"The Run itself will be worse," the doctor said. "There'll be serious accidents when all that horseflesh and humanity stampede over the line next Saturday. Well, here we are."

Henry Bowman, the owner of the runaway horse came up, out of breath. "Isn't there something I can do?"

"Yes. Bring some water and a pan up to my room," Dr. Dowell said. "I've got plaster of Paris. This man is going to need a cast on his fractured arm after I get it set." He gave Becky a quick glance. "What's the matter with you? You weren't hurt too, were you?"

"N...nothing's the matter." Becky swallowed hard but she couldn't get rid of the dizzy feeling in front of her eyes.

"Better find yourself a seat and wait down here," the doctor said, kind-like. "There. There's a good chair. I'll take care of your father, don't you worry. I'll send for you if I need you."

"That's right, Becky. You wait here," her father nodded. "The Doc will fix me up."

Becky was glad to feel the firm seat of a round-backed armchair under her. She closed her eyes. Something kept swimming in front of them. When she opened them again she saw the wife of the buckboard owner. Mrs. Bowman was slim and pretty and her stiff, full silk skirt rustled when she moved. She smiled. "You're his daughter, aren't you?"

"Yes, ma'am."

"He's a brave man, your father is. Oh, I dread to think what might have happened..." She daubed her eyes with a little lace-edged handkerchief. "I never realized that horse was skittish, and I'm sure Mr. Bowman didn't either."

"I'll never feel safe behind that horse again," the young woman said as she sat down next to Becky, spreading her wide skirt like a fan. "Mr. Bowman must get us a safer one. To think we drove all the way from Wichita—that's fifty miles—without knowing how skittish that horse was!"

"He won't be very good for making the Run," Becky warned. "He'll jump out of his skin when the guns go off."

"Oh, we're not planning to make the Run! Thank goodness for that." Mrs. Bowman fanned herself with the lacy handkerchief. "That would be the last straw."

"You're not planning to make the Run?"

"Mercy, no. Mr. Bowman and I wouldn't have any use for a homestead."

Becky looked at her fine clothes and the bouquet of roses on her hat and thought of her mother and the other women in the camp and nodded. A lady like that wouldn't need a sod house on a homestead.

"Mr. Bowman and I just came down to see the show. We postponed our honeymoon so we could watch the Run. Mr. Bowman is in the hardware business with his father. In Wichita. I brought my sketchbook and paints down. I might make a picture of the Run."

"It's different with us," Becky said. "We've got to get a homestead." She looked at Mrs. Bowman anxiously. "Do you think my father will be all right, so he can ride in the race?"

"I don't know. I don't know much about these things."

"He's got to. He's the only one in the family who'd be allowed to register."

"Oh dear, I do hope he can. After acting so brave and

all."

Suddenly Becky found herself telling how all the Fletcher hopes were centered in the Promised Land. She told about the worn-out Missouri farm with its rocky slopes and about the mortgage and Old Brant, and Sprinter. She told about her mother and Matt and Dave… and even about Gran.

Mrs. Bowman daubed her eyes with the lacy handkerchief. "If your father can't ride in the race, there must be some other way. There just must be."

It was almost dark before Ross Fletcher, the doctor, and Henry Bowman appeared in the little lobby. Becky saw her father's arm in a sling and a bandage on his head. Otherwise he looked like himself again, with color in his face and bright eyes.

Mr. Bowman hurried over to his wife. "Do you mind waiting a little longer, Lettie? I want to drive the Fletchers to their camp on the outskirts of town. I'll get the rig."

"But you don't think it's safe, do you, Henry? With that horse?"

"I'm not taking any chances. I'll rent another horse, till we can find the perfect one to buy." He gave his wife a fond look and hurried out.

Mrs. Bowman rustled up to Ross Fletcher. "I can't thank you enough, Mr. Fletcher. Goodness only knows what might have happened without you. I hope you haven't been in too much pain."

"Thank you, ma'am."

"Is he all right, Doctor?" she asked.

"As good as can be expected. If he keeps that arm quiet until it's well knit, he won't have any bad after effects. Except perhaps a slight stiffness. And the wound in his head will heal in a week or two." Dr. Dowell turned to Becky. "It's up to you, young lady, to see that your father takes care of himself."

Becky looked up questioningly.

"He said something about making the Run into the Race for the Prairie," the doctor went on. "Of course, that's out of the question."

"It… is?"

"Out of the question. Your father wouldn't have a chance in that mad stampede. Horses stumbling, jostling each other … wagons locking wheels and tipping over … No, sir. The race is no place for a man with a fractured arm and a badly cut head."

"I'll be all right, Doc," Ross Fletcher insisted. "We've got to get ourselves a homestead."

"Then you'd better get it some other way. It's strictly against doctor's orders for you to make the Run."

Becky felt as if there would never be another rainbow in the world. After all their plans, after all their talk about the Promised Land, Pappy wouldn't be able to make the Run! She felt Mrs. Bowman's hand on her shoulder. "Don't worry, Becky," the soft voice said. "There must be some other way. You take care of your father."

There wasn't any happy planning in the Fletcher camp that night. They all sat around anxious-like, wrestling with the problem, trying to find a way out.

"If I'd been killed outright, Eliza, 'stead of just laid up," Ross Fletcher said, "you'd be head of the family. Then you could take Sprinter and pick yourself a homestead."

"Don't you talk that-a-way, Ross," his wife answered. "As if the best homestead in all Oklahomy is worth your little finger. And you know I can't ride a horse like Sprinter."

"By Saturday, I'll be feeling a whole sight better. Arm may even be knit by then…"

"The doctor says you mustn't make the Run, Pappy," Becky interrupted. "You'd better not even be a-thinking of it." She poked at the embers of their supper fire. If only she could go out and get a homestead for the folks! If she were twenty-one years old, it wouldn't matter about being a girl. And she could ride—Old Brant used to let her exercise his horses sometimes. He wouldn't have done that if she wasn't a good rider. She had a way with horses.

Her father groaned. "Me, enlisting on the Union side in the War when I was just fifteen and never getting scratched. And now being banged up like this—at my age—on the streets of a cowtown! It doesn't make sense." He sighed, then turned hopefully to his wife. "Must be some way we could manage, Eliza. Reckon they'd count you the head of the family, with me laid up?"

"I couldn't handle Sprinter, anyway, Ross," his wife answered. "I'm no hand at riding fast horses. Never had occasion to be. All I know how to do is hold the reins on an old ploddy mule."

Becky knew that was true. Mama didn't know shucks about a horse like Sprinter, even if she could take Pappy's place. I'm the one who knows, she thought. I'm the one to do it. But how? They wouldn't even allow me to register.

Still she wouldn't give up. "The Bowmans said they'd come in the morning to talk things over. Maybe they'll think of something."

"Hope is a good breakfast," Eliza Fletcher said. "And worry is the interest on trouble afore it's due. Let's just go to bed and trust in the Lord."

***

The sun was bright, next morning, but it didn't shed much light on the family problem. Not until after breakfast, when Becky took the mules to water, did she get a glimmer of hope. If it came to the worst, why couldn't they make the Run with the mules and the covered wagon? She could do the driving and Pappy could sit behind in the wagon box padded around with pillows and comforters.

Of course, they couldn't take a chance of being in the thick of the race, with so much danger of a stampede. Just the jolting and swaying of the wagon would be hard on a broken arm. But they could drive carefully and still beat the ox teams, couldn't they? Becky checked herself. With all the saddle horses and light rigs racing ahead, would there be any homesteads left for the slow moving folks? When there were only half enough to go around in the first place?

No, the glimmer of hope wasn't very bright. Henry Bowman had been asking around about the government regulations for the opening of the Strip. But no one seemed to know any rule to cover this case.

"The newspaper office isn't open on Sunday," Henry Bowman said. "So I'll have to wait till tomorrow to ask if they know about any special rule. The only other possibility is to get hold of one of the officers who'll be in charge of the registration booth. Just don't give up hope, folks." Mr. Bowman took his wife's arm. "We'll do everything we can, you can count on that. If we get any news, we'll be back."

"By the way, Mr. Fletcher," Mrs. Bowman said. "We ran into Doctor Dowell this morning. He urged us to tell you again that it was against his orders for you to make the Run."

"He'll not be a-making it," Becky's mother said firmly. "We'll go back home to Missouri first."

Becky took Sprinter for a workout on the Chisholm Trail. With her father unable to ride, she had taken over the job of exercising the horse. She headed for the border, eager to see what it was like.

Sprinter ran the few miles to the border in good time. Yes, Becky decided, the Trail was much better than raw prairie. Though there were ruts in places from freight wagons and stagecoaches, the Trail was wide and easier on a horse than the rough sod.

At the border she saw that a strip of land about a hundred feet wide had been burned over. It stretched to the east and west as far as she could see, marking the boundary between Kansas and the Race for the Prairie.

Beyond the burned land the Trail stretched south to the horizon. On the Oklahoma side mounted soldiers were patrolling the border.

This north line of the Strip was well guarded. Five of the nine registration booths were located here. The south border was also fairly well patrolled. But fewer guards were on duty on the west border and along the winding Arkansas River on the east. Was Pappy right about the Sooners being kept out, Becky wondered again.

On the burned strip to one side of the Trail she saw a canvas-covered structure with several tents nearby. Riding closer, she read the sign: REGISTRATION BOOTH. OPEN BEGINNING SEPT. 11. 7-12 A.M. 1-6 P.M. So this was one of the booths where homesteaders would register! Beginning tomorrow morning...

Slowly an idea began to take shape in Becky's mind, like a seed sending forth shoots. Why wait on Henry Bowman for more information about the regulations? Why not try on her own, and not tell a soul? She smiled as the bud of the idea began to open.

Riding along, she argued with herself. What would the folks think if they woke up in the middle of the night and found her gone? Maybe with Dave for company... She wasn't too young to do a thing like that! Didn't Pappy enlist in the Union forces when he was only fifteen? And didn't his folks let him?

Even if her plan didn't work, nothing would be lost except time... "I've got an idea, Sprinter," she confided, as she turned back toward camp. "And it may turn out to be just the thing!"

The sun set and the Bowmans had not returned with any information. Becky was impatient for time to pass but she did her best not to show it. Unnoticed, she put her old sweater, the extra lantern and a folding campstool where she could find them in the dark without making a noise. She even managed to find a pencil and a scrap of paper to write a note, so it would be ready to leave under the coffeepot.

Dear folks. I've got an idea about the Run. Don't worry about me. I'm going somewhere and taking Dave along. You can look for us back by the middle of the morning.

That would allow plenty of leeway to be back by mid-morning.

Then, as if no unusual thoughts were whirling around in her mind, she began to curry Sprinter with the old steel scraper. Matt came over and watched. "You know what it said on a wagon in Caldwell yesterday?" Becky asked good-naturedly.

"What, Becky?"

"It said, 'In God we trusted and in Colorado busted. Let her rip; we're going to the Race for the Prairie.'"

"That's wrong."

Becky stopped currying and looked at her brother in surprise. "Wrong? What do you mean?"

"Mr. Milligan says it's wrong to call it a Strip. It's an Outlet. The Milligans live three tents over that way. He says it's an Outlet."

"Well, I reckon it is," Becky answered.

Becky tried to remember what she had learned in school about the Cherokee Indians. They had been forced to give up their lands in Georgia, Tennessee, and the Carolinas when white settlers pressed in. She knew that much. And they had been forced to march clear west to the Indian Territory which the government set aside for the eastern tribes. That was 1830-something.

"The government gave the Cherokees a big piece of land in the eastern part of Indian Territory just south of Kansas," Becky said. "Then, later, the government gave them some extra land… a long strip to the west, so they could have an outlet to the buffalo hunting grounds."

"Oh, then the Strip is an Outlet."

Becky nodded. "Reckon it's both." She was proud to discover how much unexpected information she had stored in her head. "The Cherokees weren't the roaming kind of Indians. They were used to farming, and living in houses, when they came to Oklahomy. The Cherokees had laws and learning and schools. One of them—Sequoyah—even figured out how to write their language, so the Cherokees could learn to read if they took a notion."

"They could!"

"They never went in for hunting much. They hardly ever hunted buffalo."

Matt pricked up his ears. "That's funny. If they didn't go in for hunting, Becky, why did the government give them the Strip for an outlet to the buffalo hunting grounds?"

That was a good question, and Becky knew it. But she didn't know the answer. All she knew was that the Cherokees had rented the outlet strip to cattlemen for pasture, before the government bought it back last spring. "There aren't any buffaloes anymore, anyway," she said absent-mindedly as she turned back to her currying.

After supper, Pappy gave a big sigh. "I reckon the Bowmans won't come today at all. Reckon they find our chances for getting into the Promised Land are pretty slim."

"I wouldn't say that, Ross," his wife answered. "The Run's still six days off. A pile of things can happen in six days."

"They'd better hurry and happen if they're to do us any good," Becky's father sighed again. "Well, we might as well go to bed."

Becky wanted to shout, "Don't be discouraged, Pappy! Wait till you see what I've got up my sleeve." But instead she yawned innocent-like and said, "I'm sleepy, too. Come on and sleep out near the wagon, Dave. The night's so pretty. We can see who can count the most stars."

Her first thought had been to ride Sprinter on the night adventure but she decided against it. She couldn't keep an eye on Sprinter every minute. No. They'd better walk the four miles. They could stop and rest on the way if they got tired.

When they were settled down in their blankets, she whispered her plan to Dave. "We'll have to wait a bit, though," she finished. "Think you can stay awake?"

"Stay awake! I'm not a-planning to sleep all night!"

Becky waited for a long time, lying there in the dark. When she was sure the family was asleep, she stealthily slipped the note under the coffeepot, by the outdoor fireplace.

"Mama will be sure to find it there, first thing in the morning," she whispered. Quietly she picked up the lantern, the blanket and the campstool, then motioned to Dave that she was ready.

They slipped around the wagon and headed for the Chisholm Trail.

The new moon was down, and it was dark. Becky lit the lantern. It wouldn't do to get off the Trail and wander all night on the prairie. It wouldn't do to miss getting a place at the front of the line.

A lumbering ox wagon was grinding down the Trail ahead. Becky kept an even distance behind it. Once in a while, a man on horseback or a light rig passed. Did other folks have the same idea of spending the night in front of the registration booth? Well, at least with the camp stool she wouldn't have to stand up all those hours, and Dave could sleep warm in the blanket.

On and on they walked through the strange, mysterious night. They didn't talk much after the first excitement wore off. They just plodded along hopefully, swinging the oily-smelling lantern.

Sure enough, others were already there when they reached the booth. A scraggly line was forming. Becky blew out the lantern. She was glad she had thought of bringing Dave. She wouldn't have liked it among these noisy home-seekers, alone.

"I've got the prettiest little quarter section in the Strip all picked out," a boastful fellow was saying. "Had my eye on it for years, drivin' freight down the Chisholm Trail. Wait till I get that there registration certificate, and I'll be on my way."

"What if they catch you?"

"Nobody's going to catch me. Not in the blackjack timber where I'll be hiding."

A Sooner! Becky huddled down on her campstool and pulled the blanket around Dave's shoulder. She didn't like the idea of staying up all night near a man who would cheat the law. But she had to talk to one of the officers in the booth.

"Durndest idea the government ever got, making us register," the Sooner mumbled.

"Just a lot of bosh," a man nearby said.

"Becky, is it almost morning?" David asked in a panicky voice.

Everything always seems worse in the dark, Becky told herself. Nobody's going to hurt us. They probably won't even notice us. Why should they? It's everybody for himself in the Run. "Hush," she whispered to Dave. "Lean against me and get some sleep."

"Why, you're nothing but a couple of kids," a voice behind them said.

Becky turned around. She couldn't make out the man's features, but his voice had a reassuring sound.

Friendly-like. "Yes, sir," Becky said.

"You don't appear to be near old enough for the Run."

"No, sir."

"I don't mean to butt in," the man said, puzzled. "But it's a long time till this booth opens at 7 o'clock tomorrow morning. I'd not like to see you disappointed, after waiting all night. You don't aim to try to register for a homestead, do you?"

"No, sir."

"Holding a place for someone else, then?" the man suggested, doubtfully.

"No, we're not," Becky answered. "I'm not aiming to register, but I've got to find something out!"

"Must be mighty important."

"It'll be the most important thing I ever did, if I can find out how we can get a homestead." Briefly, quietly, Becky told what had happened to her father. "We can't turn back now," she ended.

"'Course, you can't. There must be something in the rules to cover a case like yours. Why don't you sit on the ground and rest your head on the stool? Cover yourself with part of the lad's blanket. You get yourselves some sleep, and I'll see that nobody crowds you out of line. That's a promise."

Becky yawned. Maybe that wasn't a bad idea. Maybe that wasn't a bad idea. Maybe it wasn't...

CHAPTER 5

New Hope

The sun was low in the east but already bright and hot when Becky stirred next morning. Her arm was all prickly where Dave's head had been resting on it. Dave was waking up, too, looking around sleepily. "We're a-going to get our homestead in the Promised Land," he murmured and smiled importantly at his sister.

Ahead, some of the men at the beginning of the line were sprawled out; others were awake and standing.

The kind stranger of the night before was sitting knees up, arms around knees, head sunk on arms. Behind him, stretched a long line of land-seekers. The farther ones were noisy and lively, as if they had recently arrived and were still fresh.

It must be a little after six o'clock, Becky reckoned. She reached in her pocket for a piece of cornbread hidden there and gave a half to Dave.

More and more homesteaders were arriving every minute, grumbling at the length of the line so early in the morning. One man, better dressed than the others, with a broad-brimmed hat set at a jaunty angle, headed for the beginning of the line instead of the end. Becky stared. Was he going to try to squeeze in where he had no right to be?

One of the men ahead saw the intruder and shook a fist at him. "Get out. Get to the end where you belong. We've been waiting here all night!"

The stranger spotted Dave and Becky and moved toward them. "Listen, you kids," he said confidently, "you're both too young to register. Probably holding a place for someone else. Look here, I'll give you a silver dollar for your place in line." He held out a bright new silver dollar.

Becky squeezed Dave's arm. A silver dollar! A dollar just for waiting in line! That's what Old Brant used to pay for a whole week's work for helping Mrs. Brant in the house or for picking buckets and buckets of beans and berries. It would be the easiest dollar she ever earned.

"Come on," urged the man.

Becky thought of the note she had written: You can look for us back by the middle of the morning. If they went to the end of the line, they'd be lucky to reach the booth by noon. And then there'd be that long walk back to the campsite, and Dave would be hungry and thirsty and tired. But that was only half of it. She was plumb anxious to find out if the Fletchers had any chance to make the Run!

The stranger changed his tack. Pocketing the dollar, he took out a pearl-handled jackknife. "How about this?" he asked. "Three blades. Best tempered steel on the market."

"Becky, look at that jackknife!" Dave whispered. "I never had a jackknife." He looked at the three-bladed knife longingly. He wanted it as badly as Becky had wanted the cartridge pencil.

Becky fidgeted. Suddenly she saw Gran's face, the way

she looked that night she talked about the pencil.

"Things haven't got much to do with happiness, Dave," she whispered. Then she looked the stranger square in the face. "We're not trading our place in line. Not for anything."

The man shrugged and moved on down the line, to try to tempt someone else.

An hour crawled past and registration began. The line moved ahead slowly. Finally Becky stood in front of one of the officers at the counter of the big canvas booth. She had never felt so anxious-warm in her life.

"Next." The man at the counter had a blank-looking face, with strands of black hair combed across his bald spot. He wore black sateen half-sleeves over his cuffs. "You're not old enough to register," he said, with a swift glance at Becky and her brother.

"I know. But my father's been hurt, and we came all the way from the Ozarks. What can we do?" Becky pleaded.

"Your father's been hurt?"

"Yes, sir." Conscious of keeping the people in line waiting, Becky explained briefly. "And so the doctor says he can't make the Run."

The officer frowned and tapped the counter with his pencil. "That's too bad about your father. But he's the one to register, of course, and file on the claim. He's the head of the family."

"I know," Becky said. "But he can't."

"I can't remember anything in the regulations covering

a case like this." The man thumbed expertly through a pile of forms. Then he glanced at a page of printed instructions. "Not a thing. How old are you?"

"Fifteen."

"Oldest in the family?"

"Yes, sir."

"That's too bad. I take it your father's still a young man, then, in his thirties, no doubt. I thought I might have a head on something…"

"My father's forty-two," Becky said. "I had two older brothers. They died a long time ago, before I was born."

"Forty-two?" The officer looked hopeful for the first time. "Couldn't possibly be your father was in the Civil War, could it? On the Union Side?"

Grasping at the hope she heard in the man's words, Becky nodded eagerly. "Yes, sir. He was in the Civil War. Not for long, because the war stopped. But his folks let him enlist when he was 15… they were so dead set against slavery."

"He was actually a soldier?"

"He didn't get to fight in any battles," Becky admitted. "But he still has his papers and his uniform. Mama brought them along because she says they're important heirlooms in the family."

"Good!" the government man exclaimed. "Then I think we can fix you up. The government's always been partial to its soldiers when it comes to homesteading. Why, the first homestead ever granted under the law President Lincoln signed in 1862, that first homestead went to a soldier. Yes, sir. Daniel Freeman got the first homestead over near Beatrice, Nebraska. He had to get back to his regiment before the land office opened the day after New Year, 1863. So on New Year's Eve, at midnight, in the midst of a dance at the hotel, they opened the land office for him special to give him a chance to file… Yes—your father having been a Union soldier gives us a little leeway for getting him a homestead."

All those people waiting to register, and here the government man was a-talking about the first homesteader! Becky interrupted, "So you think you can do something?"

"Just a minute." The officer hunted for a certain place among the instructions. He nodded as he read. "This part is about a soldier registering in person," he said, pointing to the first paragraph, "and this part is about a soldier registering through an agent. That's what we're after."

Becky didn't know what the officer was talking about. The only agent she'd ever heard of was the ticket agent at the railroad depot. "What's an agent?" she asked.

"Just a name for a person acting in the place of another."

"Do you mean… my mother could act for my father… because he was a Union soldier?"

"Yes, that's right."

"She could take my father's place?"

"Absolutely." The officer shuffled through the pile of government forms. "Here's the one I want. Form 4-545. I'll have to give you two copies—one for us here at the booth and one for the land office later."

"Yes, sir." Becky's voice was full of eagerness. The long night was forgotten.

"You take these home and have your father fill them out, appointing your mother to act for him. He'll have to sign in the presence of a notary public, but that won't be hard. The clerk at the hotel is a notary, I understand, and so is the Justice of the Peace. His office is right across from the depot. Have you got everything straight? Your father is to fill out these forms and have a notary public witness the signing. Then when your mother shows that paper she can register. She can make the Run and claim a homestead."

"All by herself?" Becky asked. "Would she have to do it all alone?"

"No reason somebody couldn't go along with her in a wagon or a rig," the government man said. "Somebody else could even drive the horse if she wanted. It wouldn't matter so long as she did the registering and filing."

Go along in a rig! Drive the horse! Make the Run into the Race for the Prairie! Becky was trembling with excitement as she held out her hand for the papers. Sprinter could pull a rig. And the Bowmans had a rig they wouldn't be needing for the race… surely they'd lend it.

"You understand what I've been saying?" the officer asked. "Your mother will have to present the other copy of this when she files on her claim at the land office—the land office at Enid, probably, if you're heading that way."

Becky stared down at the precious form, Form 4-545. "My mother can register when she brings this back, filled out?"

"That's the idea."

"But…" Becky turned and looked at the long line of home-seekers in front of the booth. "Could I stand in line part of the time for her, sir? It takes a long time, standing in line."

"How did you get here so fast?"

"We stayed up all night. Both of us."

"Bless my soul," the officer said. "All night! Well, since two of you have already taken a turn in line, I'm going to write your mother a pass. That's what I'm going to do." He wrote something on a slip of paper. "You tell your mother to come around to the back of the booth with this, and we'll take care of her. Anytime during the day. I think you've done enough waiting for the family. And I hope you get a first-rate homestead."

When Becky turned away from the booth, birds were singing on the branches of her heart. Robins and meadowlarks and wrens! Even the old Chisholm Trail seemed to hum as she and Dave hurried along. Oh, what a day! What a bright September day full of promises!

Becky forgot all about being hungry and tired and stiff from sitting up all night. She forgot all about the broken rainbows, because they were full again now, and shining. She smiled at Dave.

"Promised Land," he kept saying as if the words had a good taste on his tongue.

"Promised Land," Becky echoed. Come Saturday, she'd be driving Sprinter into the Race for the Prairie! She'd be driving Sprinter, with her mother beside her on the seat of the Bowman buckboard.

Matt came dashing to meet them as they neared the campsite. "Here they are," he called over his shoulder. "Where've you been all this time?" he demanded. "What did you do? Why didn't you say more under the coffeepot? Where'd you go? Why didn't you take me along?"

Becky laughed. "Oh, I just had an idea and took Dave along for company. I couldn't very well take both of you."

"What? What was your idea?"

Their father and mother joined in the questioning. And between bites of cold flapjacks and dried prunes, Becky told everything that had happened since she and Dave had slipped away from the camp the night before.

"Here are the forms," she said, finally, handing over the precious papers. "And here's the pass for you, Mama, when you go to register. I guess that's all."

"All? All? It's like catching hold of a rainbow, daughter, and finding the pot of gold at the end!" Eliza Fletcher said.

Ross Fletcher's pleasure bubbled up like a spring of mountain water. "What's a little matter of a broken arm when I've got an agent like you, Eliza? And a right fast horse to make the Run. And a right smart daughter like Becky!"

Becky flushed. It was the first time in a long while Pappy had called her right smart. Not since she used to bring home gold stars from school on her arithmetic papers. Pappy wasn't one to go around passing out bouquets.

"It's not the way we planned making the Run, Ross,"

Becky's mother said. "But maybe second-best won't be too bad."

"With Bowman's rig and Sprinter in the harness, I'm a-counting on you picking us a homestead that will be a sight better than second-best. That's what I'm a-counting on."

Then for the first time since leaving the registration booth, Becky saw a sudden cloud darkening her horizon. She frowned. "We ... we haven't asked the Bowmans yet ... about using their rig and harness," she said.

"That's so," her father answered. "But they're itching to do something to help. You know that. They'll be pleasured to let us use the buckboard, I bet my bottom dollar."

"They came down to see the show for their honeymoon, Pappy. How are they going to see it if we're a-driving off with their rig and harness? Mrs. Bowman can't walk all that way to the border. Not in those rustly skirts and a hat with roses."

"You don't think we're a-going to miss out on the show, do you—Matt and Dave and me? We'll take the mules and wagon and drive down to see you off. And Henry Bowman and his wife can come along. Henry can drive. That-a-way I won't be taking any chances with my arm."

Becky sighed happily. That would fix everything.

"What gladdens me," Ross Fletcher went on, "is that even taking the rig, you'll still be going light. Sprinter will make good time." He looked at his wife, sober-like, but with a twinkle in his eye. "Considerate of you not to be a heavy woman, Eliza."

"Considerate of you to notice, Ross," his wife answered back.

Ross Fletcher turned to Becky. "It will be up to you to get Sprinter used to the buckboard, daughter. You'd best ride into town after you get washed up and rested. You'd best find the Bowmans, while your mother and I go over these papers. It will be up to you to get Sprinter liking to pull their rig, so he'll get you to a good homestead."

Later when Becky was about to leave for town, she stopped by the wagon seat where her father was sitting. "There's something a-troubling me, though, Pappy, about finding a homestead. How are we going to know what quarter section we get? How will we know what to file on?"

"The Strip's all been surveyed into sections, of 640 acres each," came the answer. "There'll be posts on the outside boundaries of each section at the corners, showing the section number, township and range. You'll have to scout around for the markers and copy off the figures. The main thing is not to get mixed up with somebody else wanting the same land."

***

Becky spent hours every day getting Sprinter used to pulling the Bowmans' buckboard. She'd drive up the Trail to the north of Caldwell, toward Wichita, or south to the border of the Strip. Sometimes she'd cut across country, so Sprinter would get used to the feel of sod. She didn't work the horse hard, but she was thorough.

Usually Dave or Matt went along. Sometimes, but rarely, her mother. One morning, Dave was sitting beside her on the spring seat, his forehead puckered into a frown. "Why isn't it a State where we're going, Becky?" he asked. "Why isn't it a State like Missouri and Kansas and Arkansas and Illinois and Kentucky…"

"You don't have to name all the forty-four States in the Union, Dave."

"But why isn't Oklahomy a State?"

"Because it's still too young. It's only been Oklahoma Territory for three years."

"You mean it's only been born three years?"

"Well…born isn't the right word. It was Indian Territory for a long time before that. For more than half a century."

"Oh. But when will it be a State?"

"That's like asking when I'll be married, Dave. Nobody knows."

Dave nodded solemnly. "Maybe you won't get married for… twenty-five years."

"Then," Becky said, slapping the reins on Sprinter's back, "Oklahoma will beat me. Because when we homesteaders get a-living there, there'll be enough people to make it a State long before twenty-five years!"

Soon her brother's mind was darting off on something else. "Becky, do you know Mrs. Bowman paints pictures? She painted a picture of our old wagon yesterday, with Gran's rocking chair sitting beside it. If you could paint a real nice picture, what would you paint it about?"

Becky considered. "I'd like to paint horses, but they're too hard. Anyhow, I can't paint."

"But if you could," Dave persisted. "Something easier than horses. Think hard."

"A rainbow, I guess," Becky said. She brightened. That wasn't a bad idea. "A rainbow looping over the Promised Land!"

Dave's eyes shone. "That would do!"

"Might put in a big white house with green trim," Becky said dreamily. "And a silver pin shaped like a bowknot, and a ..."

"The rainbow and house will be enough. Thanks, Becky."

"For what?"

"For the good idea."

"Idea for what?"

"That's a secret ... but you'll know long before Oklahomy becomes a State!"

Eliza Fletcher said one noon, "See if you can buy some milk next time you pass a farm, Becky. Here's ten cents and a covered pail. I'm hankering for some good milk gravy."

Ever since leaving Missouri, Becky's mother had regretted selling the old red cow and heifer. Her husband had voted against taking them along. "They'd slow up the procession, Eliza," he'd said. "Cows are poky. And their feet get sore after a while. I reckon we can buy ourselves a cow somewhere out there."

And so the Fletchers had come along with a crate of chickens, but no cow. Now, camping near Caldwell, they faced a shortage of milk and the water wasn't too good for drinking.

They could take the mules and Sprinter to drink at the river, though it was some distance away. But that water wasn't safe for humans to drink unless it was boiled. It was hot weather to have to boil water over a campfire.

Henry Bowman reported that the water problem in Caldwell itself was really serious. "There just aren't enough wells to supply all the people crowding in for the Run this hot, dry summer. Why, folks are charging the wildest prices for a bucket of water."

"Pity Jabe Storey isn't around," Becky's father remarked. "He could witch some wells."

"A well-witch would make a pile of money in this country," said Henry Bowman.

Becky smiled to herself remembering how Oren had looked when she had said something like that. But she didn't try to explain. Maybe Mr. Bowman wouldn't understand.

On Wednesday morning, three days before the Run, Becky and Matt were giving Sprinter a trot on the Wichita road when they saw a slow-moving covered wagon ahead.

"Most wagons are going toward Caldwell these days, not away from it," Becky remarked.

"I feel sorry for the people who don't drive a horse like Sprinter," Matt said. "They get all our dust."

"Here's one wagon won't get our dust," Becky decided. "I'll go far enough around."

She swung wide and took her time getting back on the main track well ahead of the ox team. Sprinter was clicking along at a good pace. Matt turned in the seat and looked back, shading his eyes.

"That man walking beside the oxen looked like Mr. Storey, and there was a boy on the seat might have been Oren," he said.

Becky pulled Sprinter to a walk. "Are you making that up?"

"Me? No, of course not." He turned around again. "'Course, I can't see very well so far away."

What would Oren and his father be doing out here, miles from town and going away from Caldwell? Becky had been keeping an eye out for the Storeys all week. But it was like looking for a pin in a puddle, with all those land-seekers swarming around the town.

"I'm a-going to turn around," she said. "If we go slow when we meet the wagon, we can get a good look at their faces. If it's Oren… I'd powerful like to see Oren again!"

Strangely enough, when Becky turned around and headed Sprinter toward Caldwell, there was no ox-drawn wagon to be seen on the road. "What happened to it?"

Matt pointed to a white-topped wagon through a fringe of trees heading toward a farmhouse. "Maybe that's it."

"Must be," Becky agreed. "Just some farmer a-coming home from town with the groceries. You and your Storeys!"

"Storeys!" Matt giggled. "Two Storeys, Oren and his father—and sometimes my stories come true."

"Sometimes," Becky admitted. She'd like nothing better than to have Oren and his father for neighbors when they got to the Race for the Prairie. But how could that come true, when she couldn't even find them in Caldwell? How could that come true?

CHAPTER 6

On Your Mark!

Friday came. Friday the 15th, the day before the Run. All along the border of the Race for the Prairie the air was charged with excitement. Becky could feel it everywhere—on the outskirts of town among the campers, in the streets of Caldwell, in the stores. Everywhere.

She heard people say that there would be more than a hundred thousand homesteaders in the Run, racing into the Strip next day from four directions. At least fifteen thousand from Caldwell, alone. Other thousands had gathered there to watch the race, or to wait for their men-folks to come back when the stampede was over.

Becky noticed that most of the homesteaders were younger than her father. But there were older men, too. And women—women alone and widows with children. "Got to get a homestead, got to get a homestead," was printed on almost every face.

Henry Bowman reported that the Rock Island depot at Caldwell was jammed and tickets were selling like hot cakes. The Rock Island had trains all ready for the next day, trains of forty-two cattle cars each. Land-hungry homesteaders would jam into the cars and even hang on to the cowcatchers, for the ride to Enid. Some would jump off the slow-moving train to stake claims along the way.

That was what Jabe Storey thought of doing, Becky remembered. Maybe he was out there at the depot now, getting his ticket. Oren would have to wait behind with the oxen until his father staked a claim. Poor Oren. What would he think if he knew Becky would be driving Sprinter in the race!

All week she had been trying to imagine what the race would be like. On one trip to the border in the buckboard, she had picked out the perfect spot on the Trail where she'd like to be when the gun went off. But how could she be sure of getting that place? Wouldn't folks wait all night at the line, too, to get a place as they had at the registration booth?

But Sprinter wouldn't stand in place all night and until noon the next day. That bothered Becky. And even if the horse would stand how could she and her mother wait all those hours? She mulled the problem over.

She didn't agree with Pappy that if they got Sprinter into position by 8 o'clock Saturday morning, that would be time enough. Besides, even four hours of standing in the hot sun would be hard on a high-strung horse like Sprinter.

Finally, Becky figured out a plan and talked it over with the family Friday noon at dinner. "It's important to get a good place on the Trail, for the start of the race," she began.

"Prime important," Pappy agreed.

"We won't get it if we wait till 8 o'clock in the morning."

"Maybe not," Pappy admitted. "But you'd be worn out if you waited in place too long, you and your ma and

Sprinter."

"I've been thinking from all directions," Becky went on. "Why don't we break camp and move close to the border this afternoon?"

Her father looked doubtful. "What for?"

"Well, if the Bowmans came with us, there'd be three of us to take turns, keeping the rig in place, Pappy. We could drive Sprinter to the place we wanted late this afternoon…"

Ross Fletcher shook his head. "I'm against having Sprinter stand in harness that long, with a race like that ahead of him."

"But that's just it, Pappy! He wouldn't have to stand in harness. After we got the buckboard in place, we could unhitch Sprinter and bring him back to wherever we camp. As long as someone guards the buckboard, nobody's a-going to move it. We'd keep our position. Mr. Bowman and you and I could take turns sitting in the rig all night and part of the morning."

"Sitting in the rig!" her father exclaimed. "That's not a bad idea. But if there's any sitting to be done, Henry and I will do it. You get some sleep, Becky."

"With someone a-guarding the rig, Pappy, we wouldn't have to hitch up Sprinter till the middle of the morning, would we? Then he'd be good and fresh, and we'd still have our place in line."

"I think you've hit on something," her father nodded thoughtfully. "Yes, sir, I think you have. What's been bothering me all along was having Sprinter stand in the traces so many hours. Your plan would do away with that. Daughter, you've got a good thinking head on your shoulders. What do you say, Eliza?"

"I say Becky's been a-doing some knocking, and the door has opened."

"It will be handier, too, if we're camping near the border, when you come back from filing on the claim. Yes, sir, it's an all-around good idea." Ross Fletcher smiled. "And sitting guard in a buckboard is one thing a man with a broken arm can do."

Henry Bowman and his wife were pleased with the plan of camping near the line with the Fletchers. Becky harnessed Sprinter to the rig and called for them and their things at the boardinghouse early in the afternoon. "This way we won't miss a thing," Mrs. Bowman exclaimed. "We'll be right in on the ground floor, you might say."

"Ground floor is right," Becky grinned. "That's the only kind of floor there is in a tent." She didn't feel shy with Lettie Bowman any longer.

"Guarding the rig is like taking part in the race," said Henry Bowman.

The Fletchers broke camp that afternoon and, along with the Bowmans, moved down near the starting line.

"All we need is a deck on top of the covered wagon," Henry Bowman laughed. "Then we'd be able to see everything when the race began."

"We'd be able to see the whole Cherry Tree Strip!" Matt cried. He turned solemn eyes on Becky. "I hope you and Mama find good pickings when you get there."

"Where do you figure the best place for a homestead is,

Mr. Fletcher?" Henry asked.

Ross Fletcher took out the much-thumbed map of the Strip, which Becky knew practically by heart. "Here," he said, pointing. "Here's the Chisholm Trail, running north and south through the Strip, going past the town-site of Enid. You see, Enid is a long sight farther away from the northern border of the Strip than from the southern. So, folks coming in from the south line will get to Enid first and snap up the best land around there.

"I figure Eliza and Becky should follow the Trail till they get well past the Salt Fork branch. That's here. They'll have to ford the river but the water will be low this time of year. Within about two hours of the starting gun, riders from the north and south will meet near the middle of the Strip—those who haven't found themselves a homestead along the way. So I suggest Eliza should start looking for a stream to the east before 2 o'clock, before the crowd from the south begins arriving. That way they ought to find a good place not too far from Enid."

"We'll find it, Pappy," Becky said, confidently.

"A good quarter section we can set to work on right away."

"But you can't do much in the fall, can you?" Henry Bowman asked.

"First thing we'll do is to plow ourselves a fire guard," Ross answered. "We'll plant us peach trees and watermelons in the spring. Second thing, we'll dig us a well. Then we'll get to work on the sod house. Oh, there'll be plenty for the Fletchers to do!"

Behind the seat of the buckboard was a small wagon box for holding light supplies. Carefully Becky and her father figured out what to take along. "It's important to go as light as possible," Ross Fletcher said repeatedly. "The less weight to pull, the better time Sprinter will make. You and your mother together don't weigh much more than a full-grown, husky man, so you won't be a-starting with a handicap. Let's see. You'll need a stake with our name and date on it and a flag of some sort. Piece of that old red-checked tablecloth would be good."

"Will there be stones for pounding in the stake, Pappy?"

"Maybe not. Most of the Strip is rolling grassland. May not be many stones. You'd best take the hatchet, Becky. May need it anyway. Let's see, you'll need a canteen of water and food... there'll be supper tomorrow and meals for Sunday at the claim. I figure you'll be heading for Enid late Sunday afternoon, so you'll be on hand when the land office opens early Monday, then you'd be back here with us on Tuesday."

"We'll do the best we can."

"It wouldn't hurt to put in a little extra food, though. And you'd best take a piece of canvas in case of rain, Becky. This drought is bound to break some time. And a shovel. You might have time to start digging some water holes, if you locate near a creek or draw. Even if the bed looks dry, there may be underground water. And remember, the more you can do to mark the claim as taken, the better. We can't afford a contest at law, as I've said."

Becky couldn't wait for the rest of the afternoon to pass. She was fidgety with excitement. "Tomorrow at this time, we'll have 160 acres in the Promised Land. But why don't we hurry and get the buckboard in place? What are we waiting for?"

Her mother went about her tasks in her usual quiet way, arranging everything for the days she would be gone. She gave good-natured suggestions to Mrs. Bowman about how to make corn dodgers and hasty pudding. She cautioned Dave to watch out for Matt and Matt to watch out for the chickens. Ross Fletcher climbed into the rig. With Becky holding Sprinter's reins they started toward the picked-out place at the border, plumb on the Chisholm Trail.

"It's not wise to get a place right at the front, Becky," her father said. "Natural thing is for the saddle horses to take the foremost places. They'll be off first, anyway, and make the best time. Just as well not to have them crowding into you from the rear when the gun goes off."

Becky had heard enough talk about the race of 1889 to know how the line-up would be. Saddle horses first. Then the light rigs and wagons. Heavy wagons and covered wagons last. "But let's be at the front of the light wagons, Pappy," she pleaded.

They found their place, and Becky knew it was a good one. Her father looked up and down the burned strip at the border. "All those waiting hoofs a-stomping and a-churning in the dust and charred grass tomorrow morning! It's going to be a dirty, dusty place to wait for the signal. Well, Becky, you unhitch Sprinter and take him back to camp. I'll start my stint of sitting. Toward midnight Henry Bowman will come to spell me. We've a good place here, and I mean to keep it."

***

Becky had a hard time going to sleep that night—the night before the biggest race in the world. As she lay near the wagon waiting for sleep to come, Becky could hear shouting men, stomping hoofs, and grinding wagon wheels. Forehanded land-seekers were already picking their places for the race. It was good to know that the buckboard was safely in place, with Henry Bowman and Pappy taking turns keeping it there. She dropped into a fitful sleep.

By 8 o'clock in the morning there was already a jam of horses and wagons along the border, especially on the Trail. Ross Fletcher came back from his early-morning guard duty more pleased than ever with Becky's idea.

"Saving a place, and saving our horse—that was good thinking, Becky." He reported that a number of other homesteaders had placed their wagons during the night and unhitched their horses. "The Chisholm Trail is a mighty popular spot this morning. Reckon a body needn't study a map to know it's the only road into the Strip."

By 9 o'clock it was clear that if Sprinter wasn't hitched up soon, Becky would have an impossible time getting him through the press of wagons and rigs to the waiting shafts of the buckboard. "Can't we bring him now, Pappy?" she urged. "Ma's ready."

"Yes, I reckon you'd better get him through while you

can. The wait won't be too long now. Only about three hours. Are you ready, Eliza? Do you have the $14 for the filing fee put away safe and sound? And your signed paper as my agent? And the registration certificate? And a pencil and paper to take down the figures on the survey posts? Well, goodbye, then. And good luck to you, Eliza. Good luck to the three of you, Becky and Sprinter included."

When Henry Bowman, on duty at the buckboard, saw Becky coming with Sprinter, he helped get them through the crowd on the Trail. Eliza Fletcher had already squeezed ahead, to take her place on the wagon seat.

Becky was conscious of a great deal of noise and dust and excitement, but not until she sat in the buckboard with the reins in her hands did she really have a chance to look around.

"A hot day for racing horses," Becky's mother sighed.

"I'll give Sprinter a good rubdown after we find our homestead," Becky promised. "Then I'll walk him around for a while so he won't get stiff. Look, Mama." She pointed, "There's a woman on horseback trying to get a place at the front of the line. We're not the only women folk making the Run."

"I'm glad of that," her mother said, "though I'd just as soon be back of the line as we had planned. I wasn't hankering to make the Race and I'm thankful it's you and not me holding Sprinter's reins."

Becky drew a deep breath. "So am I," she said solemnly. "Real thankful."

"Been waitin' long for the Run, you folks?" a

bewhiskered man in the next rig called out. He was alone in a light wagon, all his belongings, including a sod-buster plow, strapped down in the box.

"We got to Caldwell a week ago," Becky Fletcher called back.

"A week!" The man snorted. "I've been waitin' years for the Strip to open. I'm an old Boomer, I am. You ain't old enough to know about Captain David L. Payne's Boomers," the man shouted. "But your Ma ought to."

Eliza Fletcher nodded, half-hearing. She was too busy watching the young woman on the skittish gray horse to do any explaining. The woman was riding astride, man-fashion, right up in the front line.

"What's a Boomer?" Becky called across to the stranger.

"Cap'n Payne had the idea this land should be opened to settlers years ago. He started the Boomer movement way back in 1880 for getting lands in the Indian Territory opened. I was with a bunch of Boomers trying to enter in '83 and '84, but the durn soldiers drove us out. Payne and us Boomers were just ahead of the times, that's all. You don't know what it means to wait for years and years, a young 'un like you."

What a mess of rigs and wagons, Becky thought, as she looked around. Spring wagons, carts, buggies, and buckboards crowded in behind the saddle horses. And even a fancy surrey with black fringe around the top. And a pair of "chariot wheels" pulled by two horses.

Becky nudged her mother. Someone had taken the two front wheels of a wagon, leaving the tongue attached.

They'd fitted a box to the wheels, with high sides so no one could fall out. "That chariot will likely beat the rigs to a homestead," she said enviously.

Behind the light wagons were the heavier vehicles. Most of the covered wagons had their canvas taken off, so the bare framework of bows stuck out like ribs. Sometimes even the bows were gone. Anything to lighten the load!

"There aren't many women," Eliza Fletcher remarked. "And what there are, wear mostly homespun and calico. And sunbonnets, same as us. I reckon the silks and satins and fancy hats stayed behind to watch. They don't need homesteads the way we do."

Again the Boomer turned and yelled above the racket: "I hear three men were killed trying to cross into the Strip early this morning. Shot down by the guards. Just you wait. After today there'll be no more nonsense, tryin' to keep folks out of their rightful place!"

Becky saw a stocky man squeezing up to the far side of the Boomer's rig, to speak to the farmer in the next cart. The stranger's back was toward the buckboard and Becky couldn't hear above the noise of the crowd. But she could see the look on the farmer's face when he turned on the stranger. A look of fear. Hostility.

Then she heard the Boomer shouting. "I'm not givin' anybody a ride, either. No, sir. I've been waitin' years to get a homestead in the Strip and nothin's going to slow me up!"

When the stocky man half turned to look at the Boomer before squeezing back through the narrow space between the wagon wheels, Becky got a glimpse of his face. It was Jabe Storey! Jabe Storey asking for a ride!

She saw her mother looking in the other direction. Mr. Storey hadn't noticed the buckboard and Sprinter on the other side of the Boomer's wagon. He would never know… and a full-grown man would make a heavy load in the rig.

"Important to go as light as possible," Pappy had said time and again. Becky turned her eyes away.

Why wasn't Mr. Storey taking the train, the way he planned? Had all the tickets been sold? Slowly she looked back. Jabe Storey was working his way to the rear of the farmer's cart. He hadn't caught sight of them—he wouldn't be expecting to see them in a rig. Soon he would be lost in the crowd. He would never know…

Sprinter began to stomp nervously, as he swished the flies off his back. He jerked his head and pulled on the reins. Sprinter! If it hadn't been for Jabe Storey, they wouldn't be here lined up for the race with Sprinter.

Becky clutched her mother's arm. "There's Mr. Storey!"

"Where? Where, Becky? Call to him!" There wasn't a hint of doubt or hesitation in Eliza Fletcher's voice.

Becky shouted three times before Mr. Storey looked across the Boomer's wagon to where Becky and her mother were waving. A smile spread across his weather-beaten face.

"Fancy seeing Mr. Storey here," Eliza Fletcher said.

"He was asking for a ride, Mama."

"Bless my soul, a man like that having to ask for a ride!

All he'd done for folks…"

Becky felt uncomfortable. They wouldn't be going light if they asked Mr. Storey to ride. They'd be handicapped from the start. And where was there room for him? Not on the seat, which held only two. Would she have to give up her place, give up the reins and stand in the little wagon box clinging to the back of the seat? After all she'd done getting Sprinter used to the buckboard?

"How can we ask him to ride?" she asked.

"How can we not ask him, Becky? He's our friend. He must be in trouble not to have found a way of his own."

"But Pappy said we had to go light!"

Jabe Storey was getting through to them. He looked older than he had at the campground, that first night in Kansas. "Pleased to see you folks again," he said, when he reached the side of the buckboard. "But I never expected to see you in a rig. Wasn't Ross going to ride the horse?"

Briefly Eliza Fletcher explained about her husband's accident. "So Becky and I are making the Run instead," she finished. "And what about you?"

"Been busy as a cat with nine lives since reaching Caldwell Tuesday afternoon," Mr. Storey said. "Trying to witch wells for some of the farmers. This dry summer has been hard on them."

"Did you witch a well a few miles from Caldwell, on the Wichita Road?" Becky asked eagerly, remembering the covered wagon Matt had seen. "You and Oren?"

"Yes, and beyond there, too. Oren and I got back to Caldwell yesterday," Jabe Storey explained. "Fortunate I'd registered when we first came to town. But, yesterday, I was standing in line all over again, to get a ticket on the train."

Becky leaned forward, and fidgeted nervously with Sprinter's reins. "Oh, you got a ticket? You're going to take the train, the way you planned?"

"I was," Mr. Storey shrugged. "But somebody picked my pocket. Leastwise, the ticket's gone, and my wallet, too. Not that there was overmuch in it."

"Gone!" Eliza Fletcher exclaimed.

"Henry Bowman—he's the man who owns the buckboard and harness—says you have to watch out for sharpers," Becky said.

Jabe Storey nodded soberly. "That's about right. It's lucky I put the $14 filing fee in the lining of my hat. I've still got my hat!"

Becky saw her mother's face turn bright and cheerful-like. "Of course, you must ride with us, Mr. Storey. It would pleasure us no end to help you out."

Slowly Jabe Storey looked from the buckboard to Sprinter, then back to the buckboard. "I'd be as much weight to carry as the two of you together. I'd slow you up. You wouldn't be getting a chance at the best homesteads with me along."

"There's plenty of good farm soil for most of us," Eliza Fletcher said quietly.

Instead of answering directly Mr. Storey let his eyes roam over the tense noisy crowd gathered for the Run. Every one was intent on getting there first! First come, first pick. The foremost hound catches the hare! "It never struck me so much before…"

"What? What, Mr. Storey?"

"Never struck me how greed and covetousness brings out the worst in a man."

Becky felt her cheeks turning red. She avoided her mother's eyes. Greed… Of course, Jabe Storey wasn't talking about her. Mr. Storey didn't know…

"Funny thing," Jabe Storey was saying. "I thought I might come across some friend or acquaintance here, with a good team and plenty of room, who wouldn't mind taking me. And I did meet someone." He gestured down the line. "That fellow over there with the two fine horses hitched to his cart is from Missouri. He has an extra place on the wagon seat. I witched a well for him once."

"Do you mean to say…"

Mr. Storey nodded. "He didn't even know me. Acted as if he never laid eyes on me before. And it took me a good day's ride to get to his farm back in Missouri that time."

"Greedy folks have long arms, but short memories," Eliza Fletcher said. Then, after a pause: "You're to come with us, Mr. Storey. We won't hear different."

Suddenly Becky stood up. And it wasn't hard to do—though she never would have believed it fifteen minutes before. "You take my place on the seat, Mr. Storey. I'll stand in back and hold on."

"Thank you, Becky. It's kind of you to offer. But I'd not think of taking the reins. It's your voice Sprinter knows, and the feel of your hands. It's for you he'll run his best. I know. A horse is like a person: he feels things, understands things. No. If I'm going with you, it'll be me riding in the wagon box and plumb grateful to be there."

"Then you'll come?" the older woman asked eagerly.

"Thank you, Mrs. Fletcher. I will. I'll go tell Oren. He's back there, waiting with the ox team. We figured if I couldn't get a fast ride, we'd tag along at the end with the oxen and pick up what we could."

"You tell Oren to find our folks and camp near them," Becky's mother urged. She explained carefully where they were.

"Tell him we'll soon be neighbors," Becky cried. "Tell him we'll go fishing… if there's any place to fish."

"I'll be back," Jabe Storey said, "in plenty of time for the stampede." He nodded gratefully before beginning to squeeze his way back through the crowded vehicles.

"I believe Mr. Storey is right," Eliza Fletcher said, "though I never thought of putting it in words. Greed does bring out the worst in folks, Becky. You just keep it in mind, and you'll see for yourself as you get more living."

Becky nodded. She'd not be likely to forget.

"It's printed on most of the waiting faces here," her mother went on. "And you can hear it in the voices." There was a burst of angry shouting ahead.

"Those horses must have crowded over the line," Becky said above the turmoil. "Look, the soldiers are pushing them back. Well, pretty soon we'll all be crowding over the line, into the Promised Land."

CHAPTER 7

Get Set – Go!

For the hundredth time Becky took her father's fat, silver watch out of her pocket. 11:20. Funny, how even the second hand crawled when a body was waiting!

"You keep track of the time," Pappy had said when he turned over the watch, "so you'll know when to be braced for the signal." Becky had to smile. She'd been braced for the signal for hours already.

Turning in the seat, she spotted Jabe Storey working his way back to the buckboard carrying a canteen and a gunny sack full of supplies.

"Help Mr. Storey rearrange things in the wagon box, so he'll have room for his feet, Becky," her mother said. "And see that everything's tied down tight, so's not to bounce out."

Becky gave her mother the reins and jumped down. "How's Oren?" she called as Mr. Storey made his way jauntily through the last set of wagon wheels.

"Oren perked up when he heard I had a ride. He's counting on we'll be neighbors."

When the supplies were rearranged, Eliza Fletcher was

ready with a bag of lunch she'd kept out, on the wagon seat. "Let's have a bite to eat before we go. We'll be on the way till after two o'clock and that's a long time to wait for dinner."

"I've some bread of my own in the sack," Jabe Storey said. "You weren't planning on an extra mouth when you packed that lunch."

"Oh, there's plenty. There's plenty."

They ate in the midst of the turmoil, in the midst of hostile shouting, swishing tails, and pawing hoofs. "I commend rhubarb preserves on cornbread," Mr. Storey said, smiling.

"I have some rhubarb roots back on our wagon. It would pleasure me to plant a bed for you and Oren," Eliza Fletcher offered.

"Thank you kindly. Oren's partial to rhubarb—takes after his Pa."

Suddenly Becky heard the Boomer's whip crack in the air. The rig on the other side, in trying to inch ahead, had scraped the Boomer's wheel. The Boomer struck the driver across the shoulders with the biting lash of his whip.

"You wouldn't think a few inches could make so much difference," Jabe Storey said. "It's wanting to get ahead of the other fellow turns a man's mind wrong-side-to, somehow. I reckon there aren't many folks here living on good terms with themselves right now."

"It was that farmer's own fault," Becky blurted out. "He was inching ahead, trying to get closer to the line. He scraped against the Boomer's wheel."

"Maybe he was at fault to press ahead." Jabe Storey's voice was calm and a little sad.

"But the Boomer was at fault, too," Eliza Fletcher said. "He hadn't any right to use his whip. Two wrongs don't make a right, Becky. They never have, and they never will, I reckon. Oh, I'm glad firearms are forbidden in the Strip. I hate to think of all the shootings there'd be this afternoon." She sighed. "There's bound to be trouble, I suppose."

"Move back, move back," shouted the mounted guards, riding up and down the line.

11:31!

"You got the wheels well greased, Becky?" Mr. Storey asked.

Becky nodded. "Pappy saw to that."

Becky and her mother told about their plan for finding a homestead northeast of Enid. They showed Mr. Storey the map.

"Looks good to me," he said.

"Pappy says first choice is a quarter section on a stream where we can get wood and water. He says the bottom land is richer. If we can't get near water," Becky went on, "second choice is a level piece of prairie easy to plow."

Jabe Storey nodded. "I understand some of the homesteaders aren't planning to stay all winter. They'll plow a few furrows, start digging a well maybe, and file on their claims. Then they'll go back to the States for the winter. 'Course, they have six months leeway before making the improvements required by law. But we're settling right down."

"So are we," Eliza Fletcher said. "We're a-planning to have us a good sod house before cold weather sets in. And land plowed up ready for spring planting."

"11:37!" Becky exclaimed. "Twenty-three minutes to go." She looked east, then west along the border. As far as she could see, riders and rigs were lined up waiting for the signal. The tense excitement of the crowd mingled with the heat and dryness until it became part of the very air itself.

An old man with scraggly, white hair hanging to his shoulders was squeezing from wagon to wagon begging a ride. The old man's shirt was dirty and frayed at the elbows, his overalls patched. He carried his few possessions tied to a stick over his shoulder.

"Poor old duffer," Jabe Storey said, shaking his head. "He's probably always had hunger for land, a deep hunger. But what would he do if he got a homestead? How would he live through the winter? It's not going to be easy for us with tools and supplies to carry on till the first crop. There's no chance for a fellow like that with nothing. He can't break the prairie with his bare hands."

"No, I suppose not," Becky's mother sighed.

"We're not going to find it a land of milk and honey and velvet right off," Mr. Storey went on. "There'll be work and hardship first, before we can turn the Big Pasture into farms. And an old man like that... what can he do? How can he live?"

"Quarter to twelve!" Becky said, studying her father's watch. "Here, Mama, you better take it so you can tell me when it gets on to two o'clock. I'll be busy holding Sprinter to the Trail."

Jabe Storey took out his battered timepiece. "I understand the guards are to call out the time at ten minutes to twelve, so we can check our watches. I'm a minute faster than you."

Get-there-first, get-there-first, even the ticking watches seemed to say.

The white-haired man was coming toward the buckboard, Jabe Storey noticed. "Excuse me a minute, folks," he said. Gently he took the old man by the arm to lead him back from the press of wagons.

"Mr. Storey is right," Eliza Fletcher murmured. "The old man has no place here. And what would he do if he got caught in the rush of wagons when the gun went off? He wouldn't have a chance." She watched nervously. "But, mercy, Mr. Storey is taking a chance, too. What if he gets caught in the rush himself? There's not much time…"

Becky watched nervously. Out of the kindness of his heart Jabe Storey was helping the old man to safety. But would Jabe be able to get back in time?

An officer on horseback was holding up his hand in front of the crowd and staring at his watch. Suddenly he called out: "Check your watches. 11:50 o'clock!" The cry was picked up by the guards and carried along the line. "11:50!" Becky leaned over and stared at her father's watch. It was only a second or two off. Ten minutes to go! Only ten minutes… and the race would be on!

"Oh, I'm fearful Mr. Storey won't get back," Becky's mother fretted.

"He's still helping the old man."

"I'm a-going to pray for him not to lose his place now that he had one."

Becky kept watching Mr. Storey, getting farther and farther away in the crowd. She glanced at her mother and saw that her face had lost its fretting look. That made Becky feel calmer, too.

"Here he comes," she cried. "He'll make it, all right. He's got six minutes yet."

A sudden hush swept over the waiting crowd. Six minutes to go! It was a hush of tense excitement, a pause before the stampede.

Jabe Storey pushed through the last wheels and swung himself into the little wagon box. "I was afeard for a moment," he admitted in a solemn voice. "Afeared someone might shoot off a false alarm ahead of time and catch the old fellow and me in the crush. But all of a sudden I felt calm. And now the old duffer's safe."

"Have you got a good grip on the seat?" Becky asked anxiously. "Sprinter's raring to go."

"All set."

Drivers were clutching their whips, gripping their lines, staring ahead. All eyes were on the mounted officer with the watch, pistol in hand. Two more minutes!

Becky had decided she wasn't going to use the whip on Sprinter. The noise and excitement would be enough for a spirited horse. Besides, it would be better to start easy on a long race like this; the slower starters would edge ahead in the end. "Drive a horse too hard and he plays out," Pappy always said.

One more minute! Her heart was pounding against her ribs as she stared ahead. What were the guards going to do when the stampede began, she wondered? Where would they go to be safe from the oncoming horses and wagons? They'd wheel around and gallop into the Strip, no doubt, so as not to be caught head on in the race.

The officer had his pistol pointed into the air. He was staring at his watch. Staring. Staring. Five seconds more… two… Crack!

A tremendous roar, like a pack of wild animals let loose, rose from the crowd. Nobody heard the echoing pistol shots as guards spread the signal along the line. Nobody had time to wonder about all the other pistol shots in the strip—where firearms were forbidden! Noise and dust, noise and dust. The race was on! An army of horses and wagons charged ahead, as if to battle.

Sprinter lunged forward with the rest, nervous, excited. Becky had only one thought now—to keep going, to keep going on the Chisholm Trail.

As the line broke and the horses surged pell-mell ahead, a burst of dust and ashes clouded the border. The saddle horses were soon far out in front, tearing into the Strip, churning up the charred earth. Becky pushed her sunbonnet back. She could hardly see. To one side she heard the crash of smashing wheels. Then a piercing scream as the surrey turned over. But there was no stopping to help, no stopping for anything now.

The air was loud with the thundering of hoofs and the

jolting of wagons, with the wild cries of homesteaders and shots from forbidden pistols. Get there first! Get there first!

The saddle horses kept gaining in their mad dash for land. That's where Pappy would have been, Becky thought—way up there ahead, way up there disappearing into the horizon. But against the light rigs and carts, Sprinter was holding his own.

Becky saw a horse fall and a wagon wheel spin by crazily. She swerved to the right to avoid it, and almost locked wheels with a two-wheeled cart that was edging up on her right. Tensely she gripped the reins. Never was there a race like this!

"Folks are throwing out pots and pans," Mr. Storey reported. "Anything to lighten their loads. I just saw a washtub roll under a cart. Marvel the cart didn't tip over!"

"Someone will get hurt," Becky's mother cried.

"They already have, Mrs. Fletcher, and the race has only begun. No telling how many folks will be hurt today."

Becky was more than ever thankful that her father wasn't in the stampede. Pappy, with his broken arm.

A frightened antelope dashed across the Trail in front of Sprinter. Easy, Sprinter. Easy! If Sprinter went down... Becky shivered. The noise of oncoming wagons roared in her ears.

Her mother sat tensely quiet beside her. She could feel Mr. Storey's strong hands clutching the back of the seat.

A spring wagon, pulled by two fast horses, passed the buckboard. The driver was standing, plying the whip above the horses' backs. Like a madman he swerved by. Other light carts were gaining on Sprinter now, but Becky did not force the horse. He was pulling a load that wouldn't get any lighter as the miles clicked past.

"Sprinter'll make a good fifteen miles an hour if he can keep this up," Jabe Storey shouted close to Becky's ear.

She nodded. If he can keep it up. If nothing happens. But suppose a tap comes off a wheel and spills us out? Suppose Sprinter stumbles and tips us over into a ravine or gets stuck crossing a creek? Becky knew there wasn't a bridge in the whole Race for the Prairie.

To the east, through the choking dust on the Trail, she suddenly saw another billowing cloud. Not dust this time, but smoke. Mr. Storey saw it, too. "Prairie's afire!"

Eliza Fletcher gasped. "Prairie fire!"

A jackrabbit raced down the Trail in the midst of the stampede, swerving from side to side, crazed by the noise. Finally he was caught between wagons and crushed. Becky couldn't help running over the limp body.

"The fire and frenzy sends wildlife running," Mr. Storey shouted. "May even singe the horses."

The Trail dipped down to a steep ravine and up again on the other side. Becky pulled on the reins. "Easy, Sprinter." Ahead a horse had stumbled and fallen, and was down with a broken leg. The dazed rider crouched beside it, cringing as the wagons raced by.

"Fire to the west, too, Becky. Reckon the Sooners are setting fires to shield their movements," Jabe Storey shouted.

The dust was not quite so bad now that the saddle

horses were miles ahead. Sprinter was keeping up well with the light wagons. He was wet with sweat, but the hot wind blowing kept him cool.

For more than an hour Sprinter raced along before the grind began to tell on him. Even when he slowed down, Becky would not use the whip. She knew Sprinter was doing his best. Better than most!

At a deeply rutted place on the Trail they passed a buggy bottom-side up.

On and on toward Enid, the land-hungry drivers raced. But the press was thinner now. Many had already turned off on the prairie to stake their claims on the red, loamy, sod-covered soil.

When they reached the Salt Fork crossing, Becky slowed Sprinter down. They had to be careful here, not to get stuck while making the ford. As Pappy had guessed, the Salt Fork at this time of year was mostly wide and sandy, without much water, but there was quicksand. Becky saw one cart bogged down in the sand, and a spring wagon with a broken tongue standing almost up to its hubs in a sandy pool. She gave the spot a wide berth and made the crossing without trouble.

"You watching the time, Ma?" she asked.

It was a little before two o'clock, the time when Pappy said they should begin to think of turning off the Trail. Becky glanced to the east, trying to spot a line of trees that would indicate a creek or draw. It was only near water that trees could grow. Her mother and Mr. Storey were on the lookout, too, for a good place to leave the Trail.

"There," Jabe Storey suddenly shouted. "Isn't that a line of trees over there?"

The air was hazy with prairie-fire smoke, and it was hard to see. But, sure enough, there was a line of scrubby trees in the distance. They must be near a draw.

"Hang on," Becky cried. "We're turning off. We're leaving the Trail!"

Several other wagons followed the buckboard as it jolted over the sod. Sprinter had his second wind now. In spite of the rough ground he sped ahead.

Becky could see survey posts and claim stakes here and there as they passed. At one place a little tent was already up; at another an American flag waved above a stake.

"This land looks good to me," Jabe Storey called after a while. "Reckon I'll hop off, Becky, if you'll slow up a mite."

"You take this quarter section and we'll take the next," Eliza Fletcher said quietly.

As Becky slowed down, a man on horseback galloped by, followed by a cart. Would they be taking the next quarter section? "Don't. Don't," Becky begged silently. "We want to be next to the Storeys."

"Thank you, folks," Jabe Storey yelled as he pulled out his gunny sack. "I'll…"

But Sprinter was already hurrying ahead again. He was full of the spirit of the race—the greatest race on earth.

"How will we know where to stop?" Becky asked. "Where does Mr. Storey's quarter section leave off and the next one begin?"

Mrs. Fletcher shook her head. "There's no way to be sure. We'll have to chance it. Drive about a half mile, Becky." She sighed with relief. "I'm glad to see we got in well ahead of most of the light wagons."

They came to a little rise of ground and Mrs. Fletcher clutched Becky's arm. "I don't see anyone's flag. This is a likely site. Stop and drive in a stake. Hurry, Becky. There's a rig slowing up behind us."

"Whoa, Sprinter!" Becky cried urgently. "Whoa." Handing the reins to her mother, she jumped out heedless that her skirt almost caught on the wheel of the rig. In a moment she was hammering in a stake.

There! The piece of red-checked tablecloth waved in the wind. The Fletchers had staked their claim.

"You don't see another stake anywhere, do you?" Becky's mother asked as she climbed down. They stood and looked around, shading their eyes from the relentless sun. The prairie fire had not swept here. Curly buffalo grass made a thick mat on the ground. Clumps of weeds and taller grass stood out here and there. There was no claim stake nor even a survey post to be seen. Where their 160 acres began and ended was a mystery.

"I'll hunt for markers while you take care of Sprinter, Becky," her mother said. Her voice, usually low and quiet, sounded strained and anxious.

A spring wagon came rattling past. It slowed down. "All this land took?" the driver shouted. Becky nodded and pointed to their flag. The driver whipped up his horses again.

Other homesteaders were approaching, passing, hurrying to one side or the other. Becky took a long deep breath. Oh, they were lucky to have a place! A place near a draw, where there'd be good bottom land. And next to the Storey's, too! Pappy couldn't have done much better if he'd ridden Sprinter himself. He might have staked a claim closer to Enid, right enough. But, Becky thought, glancing around, there could hardly be a prettier spot than this under the firmament.

She gave Sprinter a good rubdown, and began walking him slowly to keep him from getting stiff. Later he could munch grass, and when he was all cooled off have a drink of water. She mulled over the problem of finding the legal description of their claim.

This much she knew: The Strip was all surveyed into blocks or sections a mile square, with a marker at each corner. That made the section corner posts a mile apart. Each section was divided into four quarters of 160 acres each, which meant that every homestead was a half mile long on each side. These half-mile points would be marked by posts on the outside section lines. Well, it was up to Becky and her mother to find those posts.

The flutter of something white in a clump of weeds caught Becky's eye, and she walked Sprinter over to it. A slip of white paper. Blown out of a wagon, no doubt; or dropped from someone's pocket. She picked it up and looked at it without much interest. Then she stared, wide-eyed. It was a registration certificate! Someone had lost it and wouldn't be able to file on his land and claim without it.

August Ekland, of Hennessey, Oklahoma Territory. Who was August Ekland? Where was he now? Miles away, probably, hunting himself a homestead and not knowing his certificate had been blown across the prairie by the wind.

Becky folded the paper carefully and put it in her skirt pocket. She would talk it over with her mother. Perhaps they should leave it at the land office in Enid when they went to file. This August Ekland might show up there to ask if it had been found.

On her walk with Sprinter, Becky came across a post about four inches wide sticking two feet out of the ground. It was squared off so there was a smooth face on all four sides. She hurried forward eagerly, and looked at the marking, "1/4S" was all it said. So this was a quarter-section marker. She would have to find the post at the section corner a half mile away to get the legal description.

She took careful note of the post's location, marking it in her mind by one of the higher blackjack oaks down by the draw. Then, humming a little tune, she turned Sprinter back. This was going to be a good homestead, with rich loam compared to their worn-out acres in the Ozarks! A Promised Land.

Long before she reached the buckboard she saw her mother waving and running forward, nervous-like. "Did you find a section corner?" Becky called.

"No. But I found something else. Oh, Becky..."

"What? Is anything wrong?"

"I skirted near the blackjacks, wanting to have a look

at the draw and thinking there might be a little trickle of water for Sprinter and ... Becky, someone else is on the land!"

"No!"

There's a covered wagon drawn up in the trees on the other side of the draw. It hardly shows, but I glimpsed it through the trees.

"A covered wagon?"

"Yes. And a yoke of oxen, too. And a shirt or something hanging on a bush."

"What about a stake? A claim stake?"

"Might be one beyond. I couldn't see."

"How could a covered wagon and a yoke of oxen...?" Becky began, then stopped short, her eyes flashing. "It can mean only one thing, Mama. A Sooner. Don't you see? A Sooner sneaked in ahead of time and picked this place. He hid his wagon in the trees so the guards wouldn't find it if they came."

"A Sooner? Oh, Becky, after all your Pappy warned us."

"Nobody with a heavy wagon drawn by an ox team could have got here so fast if he had waited for the signal. That Sooner cheated. We're lost unless there's a different quarter section over there. It could be. We've to find the corners so we'll know."

"That will take time." Eliza Fletcher was thinking out-loud. "And if we're claiming the same land ... Oh, dear, we can't afford to go to law."

"But Pappy says most Sooners don't really want

homesteads," Becky reminded her. "They'll clear out for $100 or a good horse."

"That's more than we can give. Perhaps we should hitch up and try another place."

"Now? Why, it's almost an hour since we got here. Where'd we find another place, Mama? How do you know we could?"

"That's to be thought of."

"Besides, we'd be getting miles away from the Storeys, and we want them for neighbors. We might have to go so far we'd never see them again." Suddenly Becky's face brightened. "Mama! Talking about the Storeys ... we've got a witness. We've got a witness that we came into the Strip fair and square and got here before 2:30 in the afternoon! No ox team could do it that fast from any place along the line."

"So we have, daughter." Eliza Fletcher said. "But he could still make trouble, the Sooner could. He could still contest our claim. A man like that would swear to anything. Oh, Becky ... and we'd looked forward so long to the Promised Land."

"With Mr. Storey for a witness, couldn't we take a chance on staying? We'd be taking a bigger chance a-trying to find another place, wouldn't we? Where'd we look? And Sprinter is about all in."

"I reckon you're right, Becky."

"Besides, that may be a different quarter section over there where the Sooner is."

"Your Pappy could stand up to a Sooner, but I don't

know what a lone woman and a girl can do. If only it's on a different quarter section!"

"We've got to find the corners," Becky said. "We've got to see what's for sure and certain. You take Sprinter and stand guard near our claim stake, Mama, and I'll go back to the corner I found and start from there."

CHAPTER 8

The Disputed Claim

It was late in the afternoon, with the hot dry wind still blowing, carrying the smell of burned prairie grass, before Becky found what she was looking for. The last corner marker—with the section number, range, and township recorded on it. She hurried back with the news. She wasn't smiling. She wasn't building any rainbows…or any fancy big houses with doodads on the porch.

"I've got it pretty clear now," she told her mother, showing a scrap of paper with a rough sketch. "Here's the section, Mama, this big square. And there are the four quarter sections inside. Ours is the northwest quarter, no doubt about that now I've found the markers."

"And the Sooner's? His is the southwest quarter?"

Becky shook her head, and her voice trembled when she answered. "I'm afraid not. I'm afraid we've got our stake on the same 160 acres, Mama."

"Oh, Becky."

"I saw the Sooner's claim stake big as life on the other side of the draw. There's only one thing we can do now, Mama."

"What?"

"File on the land first. Get to the land office before the Sooner does. If we file first and have a good witness like Mr. Storey on our side, that Sooner won't have a chance."

"He can still make trouble, Becky, if he's scheming to. He can contest our claim even if he doesn't have a chance to win."

"I've been thinking, Mama…" Becky hesitated. Then she burst out. "You're going to have to go to the land office in Enid by yourself. We can't both of us go now, not with the Sooner here. We can't give him any chance to say we abandoned the claim. One of us has got to stay… and I can't do the filing. You're Pappy's agent. You're the one to go."

"I'm afeared to have you stay here alone!"

"When we tell Mr. Storey what happened, he'll be glad to keep an eye on me. He won't have to rush to the land office to file, if nobody's claiming his land."

"What would we do without Jabe Storey!" Eliza Fletcher exclaimed. She shaded her eyes and looked toward the late-afternoon sun, in the direction of his claim. "I've been hoping Mr. Storey would walk over for supper."

"That's probably why he hasn't come, Mama… thinking we'd go short on rations with him here."

"I wish we could talk this all over with him, Becky, that I do. I'm anxious as a hen who's lost her chicks. Out here alone on the prairie. And with that Sooner across the draw. 'Twould relieve my mind considerable to talk it all over with Mr. Storey."

"Want I should go find him?" Becky asked eagerly.

"There's still time before dark. I couldn't get lost… a-keeping my eye on the trees along the draw. Want I should go?"

"Wait, Becky. Look there." She pointed to someone on foot, crossing the prairie.

"That's too small for Mr. Storey." Becky stared into the distance. With the wind blowing, it was hard to keep her eyes from blinking. "Why, it's two people, Mama. Looks like a boy and a girl. Maybe it's our neighbors on the next quarter section."

"Neighbors!" Becky saw her mother's face brighten. When she answered there was a lilt to her voice. "Go see, daughter, go see who it is."

Becky ran through the dry grass. As she approached the strangers, she slowed down. What if they weren't looking for her at all? What if they were just out for a walk? The boy, who seemed to be about Dave's age, was carrying a bag. Why would he be carrying a bag over the prairie?

"Are you Becky?" the girl called out. "Are you Becky Fletcher?"

"Yes…" Becky hurried forward. "How did you know?"

The boy and girl giggled. The girl was half a head taller than her brother, and she had curly red hair and freckles and merry eyes. She must be about thirteen years old…

"A little bird told us," she grinned.

"A little bird in overalls and a broad-brimmed hat," the boy added. "A little bird who can find water with a forked stick!"

"Oh!" Becky smiled, "Mr. Storey. He came with us! How do you know Mr. Storey?"

"We don't really know him very well. Not yet. You see, we just got here. We're the Watsons. I'm Susan and that's Lem. We got the homestead north of Mr. Storey's. Coming late, Pa knew there wouldn't be any land left near the draw."

"Plumb lucky to get so close," Lem put in.

They were walking toward the Fletcher claim, trying to say everything at once.

"How'd you come?" Becky asked.

"Covered wagon. We've got a team of real good horses, but of course, you can't make time jouncing over the prairie in a covered wagon full of Watsons and pans and kettles and plows and apples…"

"We brought you some apples," Lem said, holding out the bag for Becky to see. "Apples from Arkansas. Best eatin' apples you ever did see. That's where we come from, Arkansas."

Eliza Fletcher hurried up and they had to tell their story all over again. "But how did you know about us Fletchers?" she asked.

"Mr. Storey was up at the north end of his land witching for water when we came along," Susan explained. "Pa couldn't believe we could get a homestead anywhere near a draw, coming so late. But Mr. Storey said nobody claimed it. Straight off he said he'd be glad to help get the tent up before dark."

Lem took up the story. "He pitched right in to help, and

that's why he asked us to walk over and see how you folks were. He was intendin' to come himself. And Ma said we should take you some apples."

"Real thoughtful of her," Eliza Fletcher said with all her heart. "Real neighbor-like. When we bring down our covered wagon, I've got some nice geranium slips. Unusual shade of pink. Tell your mother it would pleasure me to give her some. And maybe we can trade recipes and quilt patterns, too."

Lem looked at Sprinter and the rig and the checkered flag waving above the Fletcher stake. "You sure got a nice place here. Ours is pretty good, too."

Susan nodded eagerly. "Pa says we'll turn it into a garden afore you know it. He's going to start plowing first thing in the morning. And Mama's going to start talking to all the neighbors about a school. And she wants you should come over soon as you can, Mrs. Fletcher. You too, Becky."

"Ma said we should come right back," Lem said, pulling his sister's sleeve. Wouldn't do to get lost in all this prairie. "Look, the sun's a-going down red like a ball of fire. Come on, Susie."

"Mercy goodness," Eliza Fletcher exclaimed, as she watched the young Watsons getting small in the distance. "We were so excited about our new neighbors, we forgot about Jabe. We forgot to send him word to come over!"

"Seems there was so much else to talk about," Becky said. "But don't you worry. I'll go for Mr. Storey in the morning. He couldn't check the markers or anything tonight, anyway. Let's eat."

***

Jabe Storey was nowhere on his land when Becky went over next morning. So she turned north, toward the Watson place, where she could see the flashing white of a tent and covered wagon in the bright sunlight. As she came nearer she spotted Jabe Storey ahead walking slowly around, holding a forked stick with both hands. Behind him were the Watson children. Six of them!

He's trying to find them a well, Becky thought. Just like him, to be a-helping someone out. She stood and watched the strange procession, all eyes intent on the green twig in Jabe Storey's hand. Sometimes the children got in the way of her view, but mostly they stayed back, under Susan's guidance.

Slowly, slowly Mr. Storey walked over the sod. Becky watched, strangely fascinated. For a long time nothing happened. Then suddenly, the twig seemed to take on life. Suddenly, it had a will of its own. With a jerk, it bent toward the earth. Jabe stopped. The children shouted. Mr. and Mrs. Watson came running. Becky ran ahead, too.

When Mr. Storey saw her coming, he waved eagerly. "Meet your neighbors, Becky," he called, beginning to pound in a stake where the well should be dug. "Meet the Watsons."

So much excitement. So much talking. So many plans. It took a while before Becky could corner Jabe Storey and tell him about the Sooner. About her mother wanting to see him. Finally they were on their way, heading for the Fletcher claim. The air was loud with the cries of the Watson children. "Come again soon."

"Don't you go worrying, Becky," Mr. Storey said reassuringly. "Everything has a way of turning out all right in the end if we do our part to make it."

"But we can't pay that Sooner a lot of money to get him off, and Pappy will be dead set against having a contest over our claim."

"Can't say as I blame him for that." Jabe Storey plucked a straw and began chewing the end of it. "Some of the contests after the first Run four years ago are still dragging on. A man doesn't want to lose his farm after making a lot of improvements. Let alone having all that uncertainty in the meantime. He puts too much of himself into breaking the sod to want trouble."

Becky sighed. "And that's just what a Sooner means—trouble."

"Plenty of time to face up to that, Becky, when we've checked the markers. There's still a chance he may be over the line."

But checking the corners didn't bring any comfort.

Jabe Storey sat talking things over with Becky and her mother at the claim stake as the sun neared the high point of its march across the sky. "As near as I can figure out, your stake and the Sooner's are on the same quarter section. The northwest quarter of the section." He stared toward the dry, caked bed of the creek. "Judging from the wagon being on the other side of the draw, I reckon the Sooner came in from the south, 'stead of from the north like us."

"But he couldn't have got this far with an ox team if he'd waited for the gun!" Becky said quickly.

"No question about that. No question at all. I know what oxen can do and what they can't. You can't run 'em, you can't even make 'em trot. It would take a day and more to walk them here from the nearest border. That man came in ahead of time. He's a Sooner, all right."

"What are we a-going to do?" Eliza Fletcher asked.

"I reckon Becky's right about you getting on to the land office well ahead of time," Mr. Storey said. "So you'll be on deck near the front of the line when the office opens in the morning. I'd start right soon if I were you, Mrs. Fletcher. That'll give you time to rest up a bit in Enid before standing in line all night. There'll be a surging crowd pressing to file on claims tomorrow morning."

"But Becky can't stay here alone."

"Don't you go worrying about Becky. She and I have work to do here on your claim during the daytime. We aren't going to give anyone a chance to think it's abandoned. And the Watsons will be more than pleased to have her stay with them nights. No, sir, you won't have to worry one single minute about Becky, Mrs. Fletcher."

Becky saw her mother's face grow more cheerful, and was glad.

They ate their Sunday dinner there by the claim stake, getting a little shade from the rig. Cheese and bread and some of the Watson's apples. Sprinter grazed contentedly nearby, making a cropped circle around his picket pin.

"I've been thinking," Jabe Storey said suddenly. "Look here. If you-all should be done out of your claim, which isn't likely in the end, there's no reason you'd have to leave the Race for the Prairie."

"We couldn't stay without a homestead," Becky answered quickly. "And how would we get one now, when there weren't enough to go around in the first place? The Run is plumb over now. All the land's taken."

"Becky's right," her mother nodded.

"I'm thinking 160 acres is a lot of land for Oren and me." Mr. Storey munched thoughtfully on an apple. "More than we'll need, the two of us. More than we can plant to crops. We could split half and half with you folks and all of us make out. Remember, I mightn't have got a homestead at all but for you giving me a ride. With eighty acres apiece, there would be nothing to worry about for any of us."

"Oh, Mr. Storey…" Becky's mother began, but couldn't go any further for the catch in her voice.

Becky flushed. To think she had hesitated there at the lineup when she saw Mr. Storey asking for a ride! To think she had almost turned the other way. She took a deep breath. "Thanks, Mr. Storey," she said simply.

***

It was a strange feeling to see her mother and Sprinter

and the rig go driving off toward Enid. Becky waved bravely for the last time, as her mother's sunbonnet disappeared behind a dip in the prairie. It would be four days, maybe longer, before the Fletchers would all be together again.

"I'm thinking we've a lot to do, Becky," Mr. Storey was saying, "if we're to surprise your folks."

"Surprise them?"

"Reckon it would be a nice surprise to see the sod house started."

"Oh, could we?" Becky was all eagerness. "But how, Mr. Storey? We've only a hatchet and a shovel, and neither of them too good."

"We'll see about that in a bit," Mr. Storey smiled. "First off though, what do you say we go and have a little talk with that Sooner?"

For a second Becky hesitated. Have a talk with the Sooner! Such an idea had never occurred to her. In fact, the farther she could keep away from the outlaw wagon on the other side of the draw, the better she liked it. But Jabe Storey had a way of fixing things… "I'm game. Though I certain-sure wouldn't want to talk to that Sooner alone!"

As they walked toward the draw, Becky saw Mr. Storey looking around. "This is a nice piece of land. Would be good to have a well started when your Pappy comes."

"But what about your own well, Mr. Storey? You can't always be doing things for someone else. What about your own well?"

"Oren and I will see to our well when he gets here. I'll

have to have something up my sleeve to keep him from spending his days catching all the fish in the creek!"

Becky smiled. The draw was as dry as a bone at this time of year.

They dipped down through the scrub oaks and brush to the dry sandy bottom of the draw, then up the other side. Through the trees they could see the Sooner's claim stake, with an old white shirt waving.

Suddenly, a voice snarled from the direction of the wagon which was backed into the blackjacks. "This land is took. You get out!"

Becky and Mr. Storey stopped. "We're wanting to talk to you about this piece of land," Jabe Storey said.

"Get off, I tell you. I got a gun."

"Just wondering what piece you're staking on, Mister," Jabe Storey said calmly. "The southwest quarter?"

A surly man with oily, hay-colored hair and reddish whiskers stepped from the trees. "I stake on the northwest quarter."

"There must be some mistake," Jabe Storey said, friendly-like. "The Fletchers, making the Run from Caldwell with as fast a horse as you ever laid eyes on, got their stake in the northwest quarter."

"I stake first," the Sooner bellowed.

Jabe Storey's eyes roved knowingly from the covered wagon to the two big oxen grazing nearby. "How'd you get the oxen here if you came so fast? That's a nice little mystery for the law to figure out."

"I stake first. I got witnesses!"

"Witnesses? Your friends on the southwest quarter? Funny, I don't see any race-horses grazing around anywhere. Maybe you turned your race horse loose."

The Sooner was angry. He snarled like an animal in a corner. "I tell you, I stake first."

"When? Thursday? Friday? Maybe even Wednesday? When the rest of us were waiting at the border?" Mr. Storey turned to Becky. "Reckon some folks don't realize there's laws about homesteading. Reckon they don't realize they can be punished for swearing falsely at the land office that they took their homestead in accord with the law."

"Get out!" cried the Sooner threateningly.

"There's not one punishment, but two, for breaking the law," Jabe Storey went on, calm as a cat before the fire. "There's the punishment for swearing falsely. That's outside. Then there's the other punishment—inside." He tapped his chest. "Sets a man crazy to go living with that too long."

White-faced, the Sooner spoke through his teeth. "Get off my claim."

"I just thought you ought to know, Mister, that the Fletchers have the best kind of witness to back up their claim. A man who rode down with them from the border. A man who took a neighboring claim and has got nothing to hide."

The Sooner glared at Jabe Storey. "You tell the woman who comes here with that girl..." he nodded at Becky. "Tell her to get out." His eyes narrowed. "Or tell her I take one hundred dollar for my rights. Then I make no trouble. Or, instead, the horse," the Sooner added. "I take the black running horse instead."

Becky clenched her hands. Sprinter? Not on your life!

"Otherwise she has trouble. I make plenty trouble. I go to law that I stake first."

"Go to the law and you hold a wolf by the ears," Jabe Storey warned.

"One hundred dollar or the horse," the Sooner repeated. "I have as good claim as you."

"Where'd you come from?" Mr. Storey demanded. "Where'd you come from to get here so soon with a heavy wagon and a yoke of oxen? I happen to know something about oxen, owning a yoke myself."

The Sooner shrugged and started for his wagon. To get his gun? Becky's knees were trembling.

"I'm going to take a look at your stake," Jabe Storey called after the man. In a lower voice he said to Becky. "It won't hurt to know the fellow's name. And maybe he's just bluffing us about the northwest quarter so some of his friends can come in and grab it. Maybe he's really staking on the southwest. The line must run pretty close here."

When they reached the stake, Becky leaned down to read the writhing. "August Ekland," she read. "NW1/4..." August Ekland! She had heard that name before. The paper that fluttered in the thistle clump! The registration certificate. That's where she had seen August Ekland's name.

Becky put her hand in her pocket and felt the paper. It was there, safe and sound. What should she do? Should she tell?

"No use hanging around here, Becky," Jabe Storey was saying. "We know what the man's claiming. The same land as yours."

Becky did not answer.

"What's the matter? You look a little pale around the edges. The Sooner scare you out? Don't take it so hard. Come on, let's walk over to the Watsons'. I've got something I'd like to talk over with Mr. Watson. About getting your sod house started."

Becky hesitated. "I… I'd rather walk back to our stake. To look around for the best place for the house." She wanted to be alone to think things over. She wanted to figure out what to do about the certificate.

"Now that's a right smart idea, Becky. Then we can start work on the house first thing tomorrow morning. I'll be back afore long." Whistling softly, he strode off across the prairie.

Becky's mind was in a turmoil. Her feet moved clumsily over the sod. If she kept the paper, no one would ever know. The Sooner couldn't file on the northwest quarter without his registration certificate, and if he didn't file, he couldn't make any trouble.

Maybe August Ekland didn't even know he had lost his certificate. Then why should she give it back? Why should she give the Sooner a chance to file on an illegal claim? Maybe the Sooner had already missed the paper. In that case he was just bluffing it out, asking for $100 or Sprinter. Blackmail!

Becky dug around among the things they had unloaded from the buckboard and found the map. She located Hennessey. It was one of the registration points seventeen or eighteen miles south of Enid. And here they were about fifteen miles north of the town-site and a mile or two east. It would take an ox team two full days to cover that distance! August Ekland was a law breaker.

Grimly she put the paper back in her pocket. She wouldn't say a word about it!

Still… Becky knew the paper didn't belong to her. She couldn't shake off the nagging thought. Did she have a right to keep what wasn't hers?

"The Sooner doesn't have a right to that claim," Becky argued. "He deserved to lose his certificate."

But the paper felt heavy in her pocket. "I could put it back where I found it, in that clump of thistles," Becky thought. "Then I'd have it off my mind."

But would she have it off her mind? How would she feel every time she caught sight of that white slip in the bushes, knowing whose it was and just leaving it there?

Wearily she sat down in the dry grass with her arms around her knees and her head bent. A jay scolded from the blackjacks. The sun beat down. The quiet prairie waited. What should she do about the lost certificate?

Her thought drifted back to the Run, to the greedy excitement before the stampede began. She saw the farmer inching his rig ahead, scraping against the Boomer's wheel. She heard the crack of the Boomer's whip. And then her mother's calm, sad voice: "Two wrongs don't make a right,

Becky. They never have and they never will."

Two wrongs… Wasn't that what Becky was doing now, getting ready to crack a whip over the Sooner? All of a sudden every thing came clear. "I'll tell Mr. Storey about the paper when he gets back," she decided. "It's not mine to keep. Nor mine to put back where I found it."

She felt full of sudden energy. She wanted to dig a well. She wanted to build a sod house all by herself.

***

It was mid-afternoon before Jabe Storey returned. Becky saw him coming across the prairie and hurried to meet him.

She reached in her pocket and pulled out the lost certificate. "Look what I found."

They stood there in the open with the bright afternoon sun shining down on them while Jabe Storey read the paper. "August Ekland! Wasn't that the name on the Sooner's stake?"

Becky nodded.

"All his bluffing about witnesses when he didn't even have his certificate for filing!" Jabe Storey exclaimed. "Asking a hundred dollars or Sprinter. That's what most of these Sooners are—just bluff. Stick them with a pin, and they flatten out like a burst bubble."

"August Ekland, too?"

"I wouldn't be surprised. A man who'd Sooner a

homestead is a coward at heart, Becky. Afraid to take a fair chance with the rest of us." He looked at the paper again. "Where'd you find it?"

"Stuck in a clump of thistles, yesterday afternoon. But I didn't know who it belonged to till I saw the name on the stake."

Jabe Storey handed back the certificate. "What are you aiming to do with it?"

"What do you think I ought to do, Mr. Storey? It's been kind of weighing on my mind."

"Some people in your place would just forget they had it—or they'd lose it again. A lot of people would do just that. But I always figure that two wrongs never made a right, Becky."

Becky grinned. "I know—two wrongs don't make a right, do they?"

Jabe Storey grinned back at her. "Not that I ever heard tell."

"I was sort of arguing with myself," Becky said, "arguing it might be a mistake to give the paper back and give the Sooner another chance to do wrong. By filing on the claim, I mean."

"The way I look at it, Becky, you'd just as likely be giving him a chance to do right. Sometimes a good turn is just what a man needs to see what a bad turn he's doing. I reckon even a Sooner has to get along with himself. Live with himself on good terms…"

"Well," said Becky, "we might as well give him his certificate now as ever."

Jabe Storey nodded. "Might as well. It's nothing you'd want to sleep with in your pocket."

It was as simple as that.

They headed for the blackjacks without speaking another word. They could hear the Sooner chopping wood as they neared the draw. "Maybe he doesn't know he lost his certificate," Becky suggested.

"Could be. Though he'd bluff it out a while, anyway, no doubt. We won't hand him the paper right off. Let's sort of sound him out a little at first."

As they came up the other side of the draw, the chopping stopped. "We've a little matter to take up with you, Mr. Ekland," Jabe Storey called out, friendly-like.

The Sooner stepped from the blackjacks, ax in hand. "How do you know my name?"

"It's on your stake, isn't it? Or isn't that your name— August Ekland?"

"Is right."

"There's the matter of a registration certificate we want to talk about," Jabe said.

The Sooner started forward full of hostility, "What about?"

"You don't have one, do you?"

"Who says not?" August Ekland put his hand to one of the pockets in the bib of his overalls. He could feel no paper. He thrust in his hand into his back pocket. No paper. He tried his other pockets. "I have a certificate," he insisted. "Somewhere I have it. All morning I stand in line at Hennessey."

"You can't file on a homestead without a certificate," Jabe Storey said slowly.

"I know, I know." Ekland's face was white. His shoulders slumped.

"Maybe you pulled it out with your watch, and it blew away," Mr. Storey suggested.

August Ekland turned startled eyes to the endless rolling plains of the Race for the Prairie. "Blow away!" he gasped. "What can I do? Is nowhere to look."

At a nod from Jabe Storey, Becky stepped forward and held out the paper. "Is this your certificate, Mr. Ekland?"

The Sooner unfolded it with nervous fingers, read it quickly. "Yes, yes. It's mine. Where'd you find it?"

"On the other side of the draw, caught in a clump of weeds."

August Ekland gazed at Becky with his mouth open. Then he looked at the certificate again. "And you give it back to me—the paper I must have to file?"

"It's not mine," Becky said. "I don't have a right to it."

"No right…" The Sooner turned the slip of paper over and over in his hand. "You give it back? My registration? When I cannot file without it? And we claim the same land?"

"I can't keep what doesn't belong to me, that's all," Becky said.

"What doesn't belong…" Shamefaced, the Sooner glanced around, at the draw, the rolling prairies, the pair of oxen grazing. For a long moment he was silent, standing there clutching the paper. Then suddenly he burst out: "I do not keep either, what does not belong. I get another place."

Jabe Storey didn't look surprised. "I reckon you won't have much trouble purchasing a homestead legal-like, Ekland, if you're not in too big a hurry. A lot of folks who made the Run will be disappointed not to find the Strip flowing with milk and honey straight off. When the excitement dies down and they see nothing ahead but hard work, some of them will give up and straggle back to the States. There's no doubt of that."

"I find a place, all right," August Ekland said. "I move on." He folded the paper and put it in his pocket with great care, pinning the opening with a safety pin. Then he looked at Becky. "You make good settler for this new country," he said. "Well, I yoke up my oxen now."

"I'm wishing you luck," Jabe Storey said.

The Sooner nodded, and strode off to catch his oxen.

Becky looked at Jabe Storey. "Does it mean ... does it mean he's giving up the claim? He's leaving?"

"Looks like it. Even a Sooner isn't all bad, you know."

"Then Pappy won't have to be pestered with a contest?"

"Reckon not."

"And the land's ours?"

"Yours to turn into a garden. You know, Becky," Jabe Storey said slowly, "Your giving back that paper made the Sooner see himself in a new light. Made him feel ashamed for what he'd done. Good finds good, my wife used to say. And I reckon there's a lot to it. Well, we'll all of us be sleeping better tonight." He looked appraisingly at the brush along the draw. "What do you say we find a forked green stick and witch us a well?"

CHAPTER 9

Home, Sweet Home

Becky was working feverishly. Four days had gone by since the Sooner drove away. She'd been staying with the Watsons at night—not that she was afraid to sleep near the Fletcher claim stake, now the land was safely theirs. But it was fun to be with the Watsons. They were like a hive of bees, always busy and buzzing.

Early every morning Becky hurried across the prairie to the spreading, sprawling piece of land that was "home." Later, Mr. Storey came and they set to work.

Resting on the shovel, Becky proudly surveyed the results of their labors. Down toward the draw she and Jabe Storey had started the well. They had dug as far as they could without a windlass and bucket. There, on the little rise, the sod house was beginning to take shape. The walls were almost waist high already. And over to the side were the long strips of sod Mr. Watson had plowed, so the building could go ahead.

To see the sod house already started would be a surprise for the folks. It was Jabe Storey's idea. Mr. Watson wanted to do something to help, too, so he had plowed the sod for the Fletcher's house before he started his own.

It took a powerful lot of sod for a house, Becky decided,

as she turned back to her work. Walls two feet thick and six feet high to the eaves—yes, that took a lot of sod.

Becky had found that cutting the long strips of sod into building blocks was something a girl could do as well as a man. She had got to be an expert at it, slicing the strips into neat rectangles two-and-a-half inches thick, a foot wide, and about two feet long. Carefully she piled a dozen slices on the canvas Pappy had told her to take along. Then she dragged it to where Mr. Storey was laying up the strips, like bricks.

"Break the joints and bind the corners," Jabe sang out, as she piled it near the wall. "That's the rule for building a sod house. Reckon your folks will be surprised, Becky?"

"Reckon their eyes will pop plumb out of their heads, Mr. Storey."

"If they don't come soon they'll miss out on the fun of helping. Seeing a house spring up out of the prairie!"

Soon... Soon, Becky's heart thumped. With good luck at the land office, her mother could be back at the camp near the border Monday night. Then Tuesday they'd break camp and start down the Chisholm Trail. Of course, Oren's ox team would slow up the trip, but surely they would come some time today!

"Your Pappy will have to get lumber for door and window frames right soon," Jabe Storey remarked, "so we can build up to them."

He had temporarily put up two poles where the doorway should be. "Folks get going fast in a new country like this. Before the Run, there was only one building in

Enid—the government land office. Now I wouldn't be surprised to hear there were five thousand people there, rarin' to get their homes up."

"Only five days after the Run?"

Jabe nodded. "I picture the town-site flourishing—covered with tents and shacks, with some real wood building going up. Wouldn't even be surprised to hear that there was a newspaper starting up already. Come on, Becky, I'll help you get a load or two of sod. I can lay it up faster than you can fetch it."

They headed for the plowed furrows. "I'm a-worrying about the roof, Mr. Storey," Becky said. "What's going to hold it up?"

"The roof? Don't worry about holding it up. We'll cut us two big tree crotches—long and sturdy, so the crotch will be about eight feet up when the pole is set in the ground. We'll put a crotched post at each end of the house, midway. Then we'll rest a long log over the crotches for a ridgepole."

"Is that why you put the door off center? So it won't bump into the crotch pole?"

"That's right. You've got a real knack for building, Becky. Pity you aren't a boy, though I must say you cut sod neater than I can. We'll lay poles from the ridgepole to the sod walls on each side. That'll give about a two-foot drop to shed rain."

"Just poles? Is that enough?"

Jabe Storey chuckled. "No, sir, 'less you want water dripping down your neck. On top of the poles, we'll put a good thick matting of brush or prairie hay, and on top of that a layer of sod. When we finish, the house will look as if it grew right out of the prairie."

She smiled. "I reckon when Oren and I are helping you build your house, we'll keep ahead of you. We'll be a-bursting with energy, eating Ma's cooking."

"Your mother will have a hard time beating that rabbit you roasted on a stick, Becky."

Yesterday, Jabe Storey had managed to sneak up on a big, lazy rabbit and Becky had roasted it to a turn.

Suddenly Becky heard a distant call. She looked up to see two wagons plodding over the plains, one considerably ahead of the other. "It's the folks!" she cried, throwing down the shovel. "The folks and Oren!" She ran to the claim stake, pulled off the tablecloth flag and waved it wildly.

Then she raced to meet the wagons. Matt was climbing down over the wheel. "Becky! Becky!" he cried. "Are you all right?"

"Fit as two fiddles, Matt," she answered as the small boy dashed into her arms.

"Did the Sooner really get here sooner?"

Becky laughed. She had missed Matt's foolishness. "You don't have to worry about the Sooner, Matt. He's gone. Skedaddled!"

"Honest?" Matt clung to Becky's arm.

Then there were the mules coming on, and Dave and Pappy shouting, and Mama calling out. Becky led the way to the claim stake, telling all about the Sooner. And in the midst of the excitement, Oren came along guiding the oxen. Oh, it was a day! A bright, singing September day.

"The Sooner's gone, the Sooner's gone!" Matt skipped around the stake.

Everyone was dumbfounded over the beginning of the sod house and the well. "I'm no end grateful to you, Jabe," Ross said.

"Becky and Mr. Watson did as much as I did. Becky's a builder—got a knack for it. Oren'll have to go some to catch up with her," Jabe Storey said, grinning across at his boy.

Then, for the first time, Becky thought of Sprinter. She hadn't caught sight of him yet. Was he tied behind the wagon? Funny Dave hadn't come on a-riding him. "Where's Sprinter?" she asked. "Good old Sprinter— finding us a place like this."

Everyone was silent. Her father sort of cleared his throat and glanced at his wife. Eliza Fletcher returned the look, sorrowful-like, but she didn't say a thing. It was as if her tongue wouldn't move.

"Where's Sprinter?" Becky asked again.

Matt looked up, solemn-eyed. "He's gone to live in the witches' town, Becky. You know, the witches' town in Kansas."

"Wichita," Pappy explained. "You might as well know now as ever, daughter, though I hate to tell you, being you're so head over heels fond of Sprinter…"

"What happened? Where's Sprinter?"

"He's a great running horse, Sprinter is," Pappy went on. "But he's no hard-working horse for a farm, Becky. We couldn't keep him without him paying his way."

"Couldn't keep him?" Becky gasped. "Couldn't keep him after he found us a homestead in the Promised Land."

"You don't have to worry about him not having a good life, Becky," her mother put in quickly. "He'll have the best of care."

"Henry will see to that," Ross Fletcher nodded.

"What do you mean?" Becky cried.

"You see, Henry Bowman knew your mother had a powerful hankering for cows," Pappy said, "and Henry had a hankering for Sprinter. So when he rounded up two good cows, and offered to trade them for Sprinter, it seemed the sensible thing to do."

"They're wonderful cows, Becky," her mother said. "You should see the milk they give. They'll give milk enough for us and the Storeys and the Watsons, too. Come look, they're tied to the back of the wagon."

Becky swallowed hard. Sprinter had run in the greatest race in the world and won them a home-place. But, of course, it was true … they didn't need him any longer.

The cows would give them milk to drink and to pay the neighbors for all the help they'd need on the house and the well and the plowing. And nothing could be done about Sprinter now. "I wish I'd had a chance to tell him goodbye …" was all Becky could say for the lump in her throat.

Dave was dancing around with a wrapped-in-brown-paper secret in his hand. "You've got to find a place for it,

Becky. You've got to find a place for it in the new house."

"For what?"

Oren was there, standing by Becky and smiling. "Make her guess, Dave," Oren urged. "Make her guess."

"It's a surprise for our new house," Dave hinted. "You thought of most of it, Becky."

"I did?" She gave Matt a puzzled stare.

"Yes, you did. One day we were driving Sprinter down Chisholm Trail. Remember?"

Becky shook her head. "I haven't the least notion what you're talking about."

They all gathered 'round while Dave undid his surprise. "There," he said, holding up a motto carved on a smooth pine board and painted in bright colors.

"Home, Sweet Home," Becky read aloud. "Why, Dave, it's beautiful. When did you do it all?"

"At the Caldwell camp ground. And at the border while we were waiting. Mr. Bowman gave me a jackknife, and Mrs. Bowman gave Matt some tubes of paint. But you thought of the picture, Becky. The rainbow."

Sure enough, there it was. A flaming rainbow looping over the Promised Land! Becky blinked. And what was that in the background? A white house with green trim and doodads on the porch, all cut into the wood and painted.

Becky took the motto and stared at it dreamily. Above her thoughts, she heard her father's voice. "Reckon we might as well start unpacking and make ourselves at home."

"Mind you don't bang something into the sorghum jug and crack it, Ross. It's wrapped in a gunny sack in one of the kettles. We'll be a-wanting sorghum on our cornbread."

"Sorghum!" Ross Fletcher sniffed. "Won't be long now we'll be making sweet'ning from watermelon juice."

"And raising wheat for white-flour bread," his wife said.

"White-flour biscuits with sweet'ning on," Dave shouted.

"And not just for company when folkses come," Matt added, as usual.

Becky kept holding the motto, listening with half an ear to her family's talk. It seemed as if she had been away for a long, long time. She had forgotten all about the fancy house and the silver bowknot pin and all the other things she wanted. They didn't seem to matter much anymore. Now there was a sod house to finish…and neighbors to help…and the good red loam to get ready for crops.

"What you a-thinking, daughter?" her father asked.

Becky turned the motto around in her hand. "I'm thinking Home, Sweet Home is a special-fine motto for us, now we're here a-living in the Promised Land."